The Rock Star's Virginity

DEMELZA CARLTON

Book 3 in the Romance Island Resort series

DEDICATION

This book is for Julie and Tracy, two travel agents in the
right place at the right time.
Without them, this book would never have been written,
for dead authors tell no tales.
Thank you..

ONE

"Only six weeks left until you get your happily ever after. Better get that arse in perfect shape, so that hot man of yours won't be able to keep his hands off it. By the time I'm done with you, he'll be begging to spank you. Come do cardio on the treadmills with me," Violet insisted, tugging on Flavia's towel-laden arm. "Pilates works your core, but you'll need stamina for your wedding night. You and James can thank me later."

"No spanking and definitely no kink allowed at my wedding night." Flavia snorted. "And my stamina's just fine. I spent over an hour chasing Mum's new, stupid horse through the bush paddock yesterday. I've told Dad to get higher fences to keep him in, but until he does, the minute something spooks him, he's up and over the fence, and I have to catch him before he runs onto the road or something. I'll talk to you while I do my stretches, but then I have to go the hairdresser's to book an appointment for my trial. I told them my hair won't curl, but David says otherwise."

"You aren't married yet? What's taking so long?" teased Robbie the personal trainer as he wandered past. "When's your bachelorette party? I heard you were looking for a stripper."

Violet laughed. "I wanted one, but you're out of luck. Flavia won't have any strippers at her hen's night. Besides, we're leaving the country. We're having a week in Bali, just the bride and her bridesmaids. Cocktails by the beach, daily massages, the works." She winked at Flavia. "Our expert travel agent here knows all the best places and what to do where."

Robbie didn't seem to be listening. "I bet her boyfriend will have strippers at his bachelor party. If the best man doesn't book strippers, he's not doing his job properly. Of course, sometimes he does his job too well. Check out this guy. He organised his mate's buck's night, but he didn't get a stripper." Robbie whipped out his phone and swiped at the screen until he appeared satisfied. "Here he is. This guy hired a prostitute for his mate's buck's night, then got him so drunk that he passed out before he could enjoy his gift. So the best man, taking his role very seriously in the most traditional way, stood in for the groom and gave it to her instead." He held out his phone for the girls to see.

Violet squinted at the screen. "Bit blurry. You can't see much."

Flavia leaned over and nodded in agreement. She could just make out the couple – one with enormous boobs and the other looked vaguely male. He wore a watch that looked a little like the one she'd bought James.

Robbie swiped the screen. "How about now? He was

really banging her."

Flavia's heart stopped. The sordid shot showed far more than she wanted to see. A girl with too much makeup and a fake grin plastered on her face bent over someone's dining table, while a man who looked frighteningly like James ploughed into her from behind. It couldn't be – surely it was just a coincidence. Some other bloke who just looked like James. James had been on a pub crawl with his mates on Saturday, not a buck's night. It couldn't be him, and if she only looked harder, she'd see that.

"Do 'er, mate! Just like you'll do your hot little Vee on your wedding night!" one of the onlookers slurred.

Hot little Vee?

Flavia stared at the screen, unable to look away. She recognised the watch he wore. His favourite pub crawl t-shirt, the one with a sozzled frog on the front, wrinkling with every thrust. When he pulled back, she glimpsed that mole beside his treasure trail that no one but she had ever seen...

"That's disgusting. I can't believe you filmed a couple having sex," Violet snapped.

Robbie shrugged, his eyes still firmly turned toward the screen. "Wasn't me. Someone stuck this up on the internet and I only saw it when someone showed Davo what he might've missed out on, drinking too much on his buck's night."

Violet's cheeks turned an angry shade of pink. "Whatever. Put it away, Robbie,"

Flavia couldn't think. Couldn't speak. How could James...

She found herself standing outside in the rain, with no

memory of leaving the building, as Violet thrust her gym bag at her.

"Are you all right?" Violet asked. "You never forget your stuff. You're Miss Organised. No one else could have handled that last ash cloud nightmare the way you did when your manager was away AND earned Rookie of the Year at the National Travel Industry Awards. Fifty stranded exchange students, all home in time for the start of term. They created the category for you. Your wedding is going to be the best-planned event since the last royal wedding."

Flavia laughed bitterly. "Even if the groom's been banging prostitutes behind my back while promising he'll save himself for marriage, like I am?"

Violet's eyebrows flew up into her fringe. "James? I don't believe it. I know that picture looked a little bit like him, sure, but it couldn't be him. He has a doppelganger who – "

"Wears the same shirt and watch, and has an identical birthmark to James?" Flavia's voice shook. "It's him. I'd know him anywhere, Vi."

Violet grabbed Flavia's shoulders and looked deep into her soul, even if the view was blurred by the bride-to-be's rapidly multiplying tears. "If it is James – and I'm not saying it is, seeing as I didn't get a very good look at Robbie's phone and it was a bad picture anyway – what are you going to do?"

"I don't know. Call off the wedding, call the police…can you get arrested for sleeping with a prostitute? I know it's illegal in America. Go over to his house, key the paintwork on his car and slash all the upholstery, then drive it into the river. No, first I'm going to get laid. Then I'm going to tell him I'm not a virgin any more, before I trash his precious baby." Flavia let out a shaky laugh. "Listen to me — I'm so angry I'm trying to plan grand theft auto and I can't even do that right."

"Okay — first, prostitution isn't illegal in Australia. Not for the girls who do it or the guys who pay them. Murder is illegal, though, and so's damaging his car. So no police and no cutting." Violet took a deep breath. "I want you to go straight home. If you want to steal cars, I'll borrow one of my brother's computer games and you can play that all night, if you like. If you're seriously looking to get laid, promise me you'll wait for the weekend, or at least until you've talked to James. Promise me, girl." Violet's eyes pinned her.

Flavia sighed. "All right, I promise. It's not like I'd know how to pick up a guy anyway. It feels like James and I have been together forever. Now, I don't know what to do."

"You and James will work this out, you'll see. Now: home, dinner, distraction, then bed. In that order."

Flavia nodded numbly. How could anyone work out a future this shattered? One thing she knew for sure: when she did come up with a plan, it would be all about revenge. No one ripped her heart out and got away with it unscathed. Not even James.

TWO

What do you say to a man who's just lost his wife?

For the first time in her life, Xan didn't know what to do. So she stood at the head of the Penguin jetty, a bottle of rum dangling from her hand, as she stared at the forlorn figure sitting on the end. Finally, she said, "I brought you something."

"You don't even like me. What are you doing here?" Jay asked over his shoulder, not looking at Xan. His gaze was fixed on the horizon and the incoming tide, which would soon turn the precipitous drop at his feet into gently lapping waves.

He wasn't seriously considering jumping, was he?

Xan marched along the jetty. "Truce, please. I swear. I wouldn't wish this on my worst enemy." No, this was exactly what she'd wish on that faithless wanker, Jerome. "Okay, well maybe him, but not you. I believed that girl was everything she said she was, same as you. I keep thinking it's some sort of horrible mistake. A case of mistaken identity, or something! Are you sure she's really…that she really…"

"What? That she's a triple murderer who killed not only her husband, but two backpackers, too? A black widow, my sister tells me, who confessed to her crimes the moment she saw the police. And I was her next target. Luckily for me, Phuong's husband isn't dead, so she's not even really my wife. She's still going to be represented by my legal team, though. The band's lawyers and PR people cut a deal with her. If she keeps me out of all the proceedings and pleads guilty to everything she did, we'll pay for her legal fees through the whole court case. And no further contact with me, ever. She didn't even hesitate. Fuck." He grabbed the bottle from Xan's hand, wrenched off the cap and gulped the contents. "A week ago, I was happily married to a woman I loved, or at least I thought I did. Now, my sister says I didn't really know her at all. A murderer, and everything we had together was…fucking fiction. I thought she was genuinely traumatised and now I'm supposed to believe it was all a lie? Fuck." He took another swig from the rum bottle.

"Your sister – Jo – she called and asked me to remind you that your security specialist advises against any further contact with Phuong. Any contact will mean she has to foot her own legal bills." Xan sat on the boards, dangling her legs over the side of the jetty. "You know, I was as taken in by her as you were. I thought she was for real, too. But if she's that good an actress, then maybe it's all part of the act to lull you into a false sense of security before she…well, does her thing."

"It doesn't matter how many times I hear it, I still don't believe it. You know she asked to see me before the police took her away? Five minutes, and she'd never bother me again, she said. They told her I'd said no, but they never fucking told me until after she flew away. She was so calm until they loaded her into the helicopter. Then she started screaming about how she'd never intended to hurt me. Her husband had deserved everything he got and she'd do it all again, but not to me. Never to me. Fuck knows what's true any more. I don't. You know how she tried to kill her last husband?" Jay offered her the rum.

Xan squinted down the neck of the bottle, wondering what diseases Jay had, then decided she didn't care right now. She drank. Burned sugar blazed down her throat.

Jay continued, "She tried to make it look like an accident. The poor bastard's allergic to peanuts, so she poisoned him with peanut oil. It would've worked, too, if she hadn't left him. When he discovered she was gone, he called the police and while he was on the emergency hotline he went into anaphylactic shock. If she'd stayed with him for another half hour, he'd be dead, but she ran, like she panicked. She must've driven for days without sleep to get here in the time she did. Makes me think she was right and the bastard did deserve whatever he got." Jay's fist pounded the boards. "I don't care what anyone says. I know what I saw. The fear in her eyes was real. Just like the look in Angel's eyes. You can't fake that."

"So what are you going to do?" The moment the words were out of her mouth, Xan regretted them. What could he do?

Jay's lips lifted in a mirthless grin. "Do what she wants. Give her the best lawyers money can buy and hope they can help her. And…stay away from her, because that's what she wants. Wouldn't be the first time a rape survivor threatened me with death or permanent injury. I should be used to it by now. But even if everything's true, I could never trust her again, because in the back of my mind, I'll always wonder…" He snatched back the bottle and chugged it, then wiped his mouth on the back of his hand. "I don't want to die. There's shit I haven't done yet. Like get married, seeing as the first time didn't count."

Xan's heart breathed a sigh of relief. She'd done her bit and talked him off the proverbial ledge, even if his backside hadn't budged. Now she could go back to disliking him as wholeheartedly as before. "Maybe next time you should try finding a girl who isn't married and hasn't killed anyone, or at least ask her first."

Jay snorted. "When she could lie? I'd need a fucking virgin. Even then, she still might be a murderer."

Xan shrugged. "Love's always a gamble. Sometimes you win, sometimes you lose." Yes, Jay had had monumentally bad luck lately, but he'd still come out on top. Damn it, why couldn't it be her turn to win for once? She wished Jay good night and headed for the hotel manager's house on the other side of the lagoon. Tonight she'd cook her own dinner. She didn't feel cheerful enough to brave the staff dining room with her heart so heavy. Maybe she'd break out some more of that rum for herself, because the little, nagging voice in her head insisted that if someone with all Jay's rock star charms couldn't be lucky in love, what hope did she have in finding a happily ever after?

THREE

"Morning, Vee. How are your plans for the perfect wedding coming?" James' half-asleep morning voice sounded sexier than it had any right to. Especially when she was mad at him.

"Fine," Flavia lied. What else could she answer? It wasn't like she could say she'd seen a video of him having sex with a prostitute, so she hadn't done a thing about their wedding. She'd been too busy exploring options for revenge. True to her promise to Violet, she hadn't yet decided on a plan.

She'd waited all week until she felt her fury had simmered down enough for her to be civil on the phone. Only now could she say calmly, "Are you coming up today? I really want to see you."

"Aww, I miss you, too, Vee. No can do. I have to go to the auto auction today. There's a few clapped-out classics the boss wants me to keep an eye out for — ones that were stolen and trashed. He figures they'll go for a steal and we can use the parts for our other clients." The passion in James' voice was unmistakeable. If only he loved her half as much as he loved classic cars.

"Tomorrow, then?" she persisted. She couldn't ask him over the phone. She needed to look into his eyes and know he wasn't lying when he told her the man banging the prostitute in the video wasn't him.

"Sorry, nope. Tomorrow I have to pick up whatever we win in the auction. Dazza's got the lift truck booked, because he's hoping to pick up one of the repossessed cars they're selling at the auction. A Holden, of all things. I've told him, he should be looking at classic Fords, like my Fairlane, but noooo…he wants that bloody Holden. I told him it's only the insurance company write-offs that go for a song, and he'll have to pay a premium if he wants the pristine queen of someone's private collection."

Pristine queen? An idea began to form in Flavia's mind. "What do you mean?"

"He's got his eye on this Sandman. Beautiful car, for a Holden. Seized by the police on her maiden voyage, speeding down the freeway. I bet the owner's pissed. Outside, the paint's red as the devil when he's wet and under the bonnet…shit, the devil himself would cream at the power. Brand-new everything and the sound of that engine…the vibration alone makes chicks' clothes fall off." James snorted. "Every man under fifty will want that baby and the bidding will go sky-high. Ha, I bet a few babies have been conceived in the back of that. Panel van big enough to stretch out in. It's a shagging wagon for sure. Alloy wheels, custom paint job, exhaust that you'll feel in your bones before you hear it..."

As James waxed lyrical about a car Flavia couldn't care less about, her mind drifted into the realm of possibilities. Auctions, bidding wars and maidens. It was perfect.

"How'd your pub crawl go last week?" she blurted out. "Did it go off with a bang, like you said it would?"

Silence for a moment. Finally, James said, "You mean the one for Davo? I left early. I wasn't feeling the best, so I had one drink, but I went home after the first pub."

On Sunday, he'd said he couldn't come over because he'd had a hangover from drinking too much. Flavia smelt a rat. One who wore James' favourite deodorant.

"Oh. One of the guys at the gym said he saw you with them pretty late. He said you were all drunk."

James hesitated for much too long before he let out a shaky laugh that sounded forced. "Nah, I was sick. Flu."

Liar. When James had the flu, he always called her to take care of him. His flu bouts never lasted less than a week. The bastard had slept with that prostitute and now he was lying to her about it.

Flavia opened her mouth to spit out her accusation.

"Anyway, gotta go, Vee, or I'll be late to the auction. See you next weekend, maybe." James ended the call without waiting for her to say goodbye.

Or good riddance.

If James wanted an auction, she'd give him one. A bidding war from every man under fifty? Bring it on. She'd make his precious cars look cheap by comparison.

FOUR

Jason climbed into the helicopter, feeling a momentary pang when he remembered the last time he'd flown with Phuong. The pilot had told him there was no sex allowed in the helicopter. Well, fuck it, Jason decided. One day he was going to have sex in a fucking helicopter. He was a member of the mile high club many times over. That meant…special privileges, or some shit like that. Fucking helicopter sex, at the least. But not with Phuong, and not with the pilot, either.

"Morning, Mr Felix," Shou said easily over his shoulder. "Urgent business on the mainland today?"

"Yeah. Need to buy eggs. It's not Easter without chocolate."

Shou laughed. "What, the Easter Bunny doesn't stop at Romance Island Resort? You should get that hot hotel manager to look into it. If anyone can persuade a busy bunny to rearrange his schedule, it's her."

Hot hotel manager? Did he mean Xan? "No rabbits allowed at the resort. The island's an A-class reserve. No pets." Jason stared moodily out the window at the lagoon as they rose above the tree canopy.

"Pity. I'd pet her, though." Shou jerked his chin at the lagoon, where someone was swimming. "Have you seen her in a bikini?"

Jason shifted in his seat, unable to stop the image that came to mind. Xan looking hot as hell in a clinging, wet bikini on her veranda. Yeah, she had bigger boobs than he usually liked, but for a moment there, he'd seriously considered…

"She took me for a snorkelling tour in the lagoon last week. It was hard to keep my eyes on the fish, let me tell you," the pilot continued as he arced around, setting a course for Broome. Mercifully, he shut up about Xan to talk to the tower at Broome Airport about his flight plan.

A writhing snake awoke in Jason's belly. How come the hotel manager had taken the helicopter pilot for a tour of the lagoon but never offered him one? He was the owner of the hotel, for fuck's sake. Shouldn't he be the first to get up close and personal with the fish?

The fish. Not the frigid manager with the big boobs. She definitely wasn't his type.

What was the pilot saying?

"There's a chocolate beer at the brewery?" Jason interrupted.

"Sort of. It's a dark lager, but it tastes like chocolate. Stop by while you're in town and have a taste. You'll want more, I swear." Shou laughed. "Good thing it's still the wet season. You're my only passenger today, so if you bring back a couple of cases, there's plenty of room in my baby for good beer." He patted the…did you still call it a dashboard, when it was a helicopter and not a car? Whatever. Now Shou was stroking it.

Jason shrugged. "We'll see. Easter eggs and chocolate beer might make for a good Easter weekend."

Better than spending it with family. All that sympathy and pity over being fooled by Phuong – or at least that's how Jo had put it when she'd insisted he come home for Easter. Mum would worry about him. Dad would mutter something about Sharon Stone and red back spiders, like he usually did when Jason so much as hinted at romantic commitment. All three of them had pleaded for him to return to Perth for the Easter weekend.

No fucking way. He'd spend the time alone on his private island paradise with Xan the manager who was infinitely better company because she didn't have a sympathetic bone in her body. Nothing cheered him up as much as getting her riled. She was so easy to piss off, too. All he had to do was pass out drunk somewhere public. He'd take a fight over pity any day. Maybe he should get her something for Easter. Something for all the staff working the long weekend.

After he'd been to the pub, though. Chocolate would melt quickly in this tropical heat.

The helicopter landed and Jason headed to the counter to collect the keys to his ride. As he closed the door of his hire car on the humidity, he paused to wonder why he had such bad luck in love. First Angel, then Audra, then Phuong…was he just fucked when it came to women? He could have anyone he wanted for a night, but for more than that…what the fuck was wrong with wanting happily ever after? Didn't rock stars deserve it? Didn't he fucking deserve it? All the chicks in books got happy endings. Why not him?

Maybe Xan was right. He needed to find a virgin.

He snorted. What was he supposed to do – find some chick who'd never had sex, say, "Hi, I'm Jay Felix, rock god. Want to come back to my place so I can pop your cherry?"

He'd never looked for a virgin before. Never wanted to, either. Oh, he'd had his fair share of them, but they definitely weren't his favourite. Girls were nervous before their first time and clingy afterwards – neither of which were his style.

Nah. Xan couldn't be right. Not with all the other crazy stuff she thought. She'd told him to drink less and to stop skinnydipping in the lagoon. Both stupid ideas. What was the point in owning an island in paradise if you couldn't get drunk and swim naked whenever you wanted?

But to get drunk he needed alcohol and the best place to get beer was a brewery, so that's where he headed. Jason strode through the beer garden without looking at anything but his destination: the bar. Anywhere else held memories he didn't want to revisit right now. Soon, he had a pint of what looked like Guinness but smelled like chocolate in his hand. It slid down his throat like…well, liquid chocolate. Or beer. Because it was both, he set the empty glass on the counter and called for another.

The second went almost as fast as the first. It was hot, Jason reasoned, and a man needed to drink a lot to keep from dehydrating. Or melting. Or something. That's why he needed another pint. Cold and smooth and…weird how the beer tasted like chocolate. Better have another one to make sure.

Why was he here again?

Jason peered blearily at the menu board above the bar, but the coloured chalk swirls blurred into an unreadable mess. He signalled to the barman. "I need two…no, make it three cases of this stuff to take home. In my car. Helicopter." He pondered a moment. Didn't Easter have four days? "No. Four cases of beer. Don't want to run out." He drained his glass. "And one more for the road."

All too soon, he clunked another empty pint glass on the bar mat. Jason wiped his mouth with the back of his hand and squinted at the stacked boxes beside him.

"If you're ready to go, mate, I'll help you carry these out to the car," the barman said cheerfully, tipping his trolley up. Eight dozen bottles of beer clinked in their boxes. Music to Jason's ears.

"Yeah," Jason said, pointing out the door. "M'car's out there." He ambled down the veranda steps, while the barman wheeled his beer down the ramp.

A short time later, when the boxes were secure in the boot of Jason's hire car, he climbed into the driver's seat and fumbled for his keys.

"You sure you're all right to drive, mate?" the barman asked.

Jason waved a flippant hand. "No worries. I only had a couple." But he wasn't part of a couple any more, his brain registered foggily. Or even a band. He was a single. The first time he came to this pub, he'd been mobbed by girls, but today not a single one had approached him. See how far he'd fallen. From married rock god to lonely loser. Fuck that for a joke. The car's engine roared under his lead foot, as ready to leave the pub behind as he was.

The tide was out in Roebuck Bay, baring creamy sand as smooth as a hot chick's chest. Fuck, he needed to find some action soon if even the bloody beach got him turned on.

The supermarket. Five…maybe ten minutes in the supermarket, and he'd be sorted. That's all it would take before some girl's eye would get that excited spark of recognition as she realised she was in the presence of a rock god. That one spark was all he needed – no fan could resist his rock star charms. He'd take her to a hotel room here on the mainland and give her a night she'd never forget.

Fuck yeah.

If only he could forget Phuong as easily. The sweet, frightened girl whose smile lit up his world, or the calculating killer, waiting for her chance to take his life and everything he owned? If she hadn't confessed to the police, he never would have believed it. But now…

What was that weird chiming noise? Was there a vibrator in his pocket? How the hell did he get a…

Phone. Oh yeah, there was mobile phone access in town. He'd forgotten his own ringtone, it'd been so long since he'd heard it.

He cleared his throat, channelling deep and sexy. "Hello?"

"Finally! Jay, it's Victoria. Why won't you answer your phone? I've had every major label hammering me day and night to sign you. Band, solo artist…they don't care. All they want is Jay Felix."

He'd never been so happy to hear the band manager's

voice. His heart leaped…and nosedived. The world might think they wanted Jay Felix, but what they really wanted was Angel's music. He was just the front man, the face of the band. Stupid and useless and easy prey for black widows. "I don't know." How did his voice come out sounding so weak and weedy?

"What do you mean, you don't know? Have you found a new agent? Is that what it is?" Victoria's voice rose in panic.

"No, I just…" Can't write songs? Don't think I'm good enough for a solo career? Can't perform without Angel, my muse, telling me backstage she'll kick my arse if I mess up? Can't sing about love when my life's going to shit?

A police siren arced up behind him, so loud he couldn't hear what Victoria was saying any more. Jason glanced in his rear vision mirror, wondering what the idiot had done to be caught by the police. Only…there was no other car to be seen, except the police car. Both the driver and passenger were gesturing for him to pull off the road.

What the fuck? He wasn't even speeding. Sighing, he slowed to a stop and watched the cop approaching his window.

"Gotta go," he said curtly, ending the call before Victoria could say goodbye.

"Sir, could you please…" The policewoman stopped and took off her sunglasses. "Oh, it's you."

Not the spark of recognition he wanted, but Jason knew how to use it to his advantage. He looked her up and down. There was something seriously hot about a woman in uniform. Especially one with handcuffs.

"Having second thoughts, are you? I mean, you did have me handcuffed to a bed last time we met. I won't say no to a little kink with the right woman." Jason winked and was rewarded with her faint blush. "I mean, it's not like I've done anything wrong here." He gestured at the dashboard.

"Nothing wrong?" she sputtered. "You were driving erratically on the wrong side of the road, talking on your mobile phone. And is that…are you drunk?"

"Nope," he replied cheerfully.

This didn't seem to faze her in the slightest. "I'm going to breath test you anyway. You won't get away with drink driving like you did last time."

Minutes passed while Jason blew dutifully into the breathalyser, then repeated the test, as the policewoman's brows knitted together.

"Happy now?" he drawled.

"Absolutely. I wanted to be certain. You have just lost your licence for the next six months, and when the office processes all this, you'll get another five months after that. It could be a year before you're allowed on the streets again."

"What?" Jason yelped. "But I'm not drunk! I only had a couple!"

"A couple of bottles. Says here that you're 0.082, well over the legal limit. If you like, I can take you to the hospital and let them do a blood test."

Blood? No, he'd faint. Or throw up. Or both. Rock gods didn't have shameful secrets like being afraid of the sight of blood. "If I agree to go on just the breath test, will you use those handcuffs on me tonight?" He threw in a lazy smile to underline the invitation.

Instead of responding, she continued tapping the tablet in her hands as her face reddened.

Inwardly, Jason cheered his victory. He knew she had a thing for him!

"There. Three fines. One for driving under the influence of alcohol, well over the legal limit. One for using your mobile phone while driving. And a third fine for not wearing a seat belt." She triumphantly thrust the papers at his face.

"Talking on the phone's illegal now?" He snatched the fines and scanned them. "And it's six demerit points? How is talking worse than speeding?"

"It's not. But with the long weekend coming up, you get double demerit points. So instead of just the dozen you'd get on a normal day, today you get two for the price of one."

"It's not Easter yet. It's just a normal Friday."

"Check your calendar, Mr Felix. The first weekend in March is the Labour Day weekend here. The double demerit period started at midnight last night, like always. You're in Western Australia now." She looked far too smug.

"So your plan is to take me to the police station, give me a nice cosy little cell, and keep me captive for the whole long weekend?"

From her shocked expression, Jason decided he'd guessed right.

He winked. "Bring it on, baby. A bit of kink never hurt anyone. Sounds like a fun weekend. I hope you're wearing hot lingerie under that uniform, though, because if I'm going to submit to a policewoman dominatrix, you'd better make it worth my while."

She turned on her heel and walked away without a word.

Jason rubbed his hands together. One of his fantasies

coming true – that was definitely worth losing his licence. He could afford to hire a chauffeur to do his driving for him.

"Please get out of the car, sir, and give me the keys."

Jason stared at the male police officer. "Now, I was just discussing that with your colleague over there. I'd prefer to speak to her."

The man laughed. "Yeah, Nelson said that. She also said that you're the first offender who's made her want to deliver a bit of police brutality. So I'm going to use a bit of officers' discretion and give you a lift to the airport, where you can hop on a plane out of here, or you can come with us back to the police station where we'll put you in the cooling-off cell. You can spend the whole weekend surrounded by all the vomiting drunks we pick up over the next three days before she calls the media to tell them who we have in the cells."

Fuck that. "Helicopter. I have a helicopter waiting at the airport to take me back to my island," Jason snapped.

"Well, aren't you lucky? A word to the wise, then, mate. You might want to stay on that island for a while, until Constable Nelson's simmered down. The Cape Leveque Road's her beat, so staying off the mainland's your best bet to keep your balls, mate. Not that I told you that."

Grumpily, Jason shoved his keys at the police officer and climbed out. The policewoman wanted him – he knew it. Not his fault she was too shy to take him up on his offer.

Jason maintained his grumpy silence for the short drive to the airport, the wait for Shou the pilot to get back from lunch, and the trek across the tarmac to the waiting helicopter. Luckily, he still had the beer. He could get properly drunk later on the stuff. Fuck Easter eggs when you could have chocolate beer.

"Pissed off the police in town, have you?" Xan greeted him as his shoes thumped onto the resort's helipad.

Jason shot her a sour look. "How the fuck did you find out?"

"Naomi called, and said she'd booked you drink driving. I get that you're upset over losing your wife, but you can't go getting drunk in the middle of town first thing in the morning, then drive past the police station and not expect to get caught. Much though I hate to say it, you're better off doing that here until you're not so depressed and – "

Sympathy. He could take anything but that. "I am not upset, or depressed, or feeling any fucking thing at all to do with that lying, murdering bitch! I went to town for a drink and a fuck because I'm a fucking rock star and that's what rock stars do for fun!"

Xan snorted. "Well, Mr Rock Star, looks like you'll have to find some different fun to keep you occupied."

That wouldn't be a problem. He had a whole island almost entirely to himself, aside from a few hotel staff, until peak season started and the place would be full of guests again. Boredom and rock stars was like…rock stars and celibacy. It just didn't happen. Not in Jay Felix's world. Between his money and his body, Jay could get anything he wanted. Or so he thought.

FIVE

Violet took an inordinately long time reading through the auction description. So long that she made butterflies take flight in Flavia's tummy. What if this turned out to be a terrible mistake?

"Don't you think this is a bit extreme?" Violet said.

"No. It's justice. We both promised we'd wait. If he's going to throw that all away and pay some girl for sex, then I'm going to do the opposite."

Violet frowned. "The opposite would be joining a convent, not a brothel. If you do this, it'll make you a prostitute. A hooker."

"I'm a working woman already. So are you. We sell the services our bodies provide no matter what job we're doing. My fingers on the keyboard, my mouth to talk to clients, my —"

"Yeah, but you're not doing it naked, are you?" Violet

24

interrupted. "This is a lot more personal than booking people's flights. Some stranger will be touching you, inside you."

"Better than James, now I know where his dick's been."

"Have you spoken to him yet?"

Flavia nodded. "I asked him about last weekend. Even though he told me last Sunday he had a hangover, now he's changed his story to how he left the pub crawl early with the flu. I know he's lying. And if he's lying to me about this, how many other things has he lied about? How many other girls has he slept with? I can't marry him, Vi. I can't marry a man I don't trust."

"So don't marry him. Break off the engagement, call off the wedding, and save yourself for someone else," Violet replied, popping a couple of nuts in her mouth.

"I don't want to save myself for anyone. The only reason I did was because his family's religious and that's what James wanted. A virgin bride, so that's what I intended to be. Now…screw him. Screw his whole family. Not literally, of course. If that hypocrite gets to have sex while I have to stay chaste…to hell with that. I don't want to spend my wedding night in pain. Let some stranger have the dubious pleasure of deflowering me. A man I'll never have to see again." Flavia forced her breathing to slow. "I could just go out and screw the first man I meet in a pub. I could. But this way…it's a statement. It puts a number on just how much James is throwing away."

Violet made a derisive sound in her throat. "A price on your body, you mean. You're worth more than however many dollars you get offered for this…insanity, Flavia. I mean, how much do you expect anyone to pay for…what are you offering? One quick fuck?"

Flavia winced, but she steeled herself into acceptance. Violet was right. Sex with a stranger wasn't making love. It would be one quick fuck. Over and done with as quickly as possible, so as not to prolong her pain. "One night. One night with me in a five-star hotel. I'd walk in a virgin, and walk out...a woman." It actually sounded tempting when she put it like that.

"One night? How much do you expect to get for that? Even Julia Roberts in *Pretty Woman* only got $300."

Flavia was ready for this one. "I'd say prices have gone up since that movie came out. A model in Brazil auctioned her virginity. For one night, some guy paid $800,000."

Violet whistled. "That sort of money could set you up for life. You could buy a house and still not need to work for a decade. But she's a famous model, I guess, not a travel agent from York."

"They don't know that. All the info they have is that picture you took of me at Cottesloe Beach last summer. No name, no address, no face, no phone number...even a new email address that I only created today. No one will know who I am." Flavia straightened smugly. "I've thought of everything."

"For that price, what if he wants kinky stuff? Or what if he's some full-blown, sadistic psycho who wants to chain you up in his basement?" Violet ventured.

"He'd need to provide a full police clearance. A national one. One that says he's never been charged or convicted for any offense anywhere in Australia. And I'm not going anywhere near his house, basement or no basement. Five-star hotel, remember? In Western Australia. We'd both sign confidentiality agreements and agree to have no contact after that night. Simple."

Violet bit her lip so hard it bled. "Please don't do it. This is crazy. You're crazy. It's five weeks before your wedding and you're getting cold feet. That's normal. You and James will work this out and –"

"We won't," Flavia interrupted, slamming her hands down on the desk. "But if by some miracle it was his identical twin, lost at birth, who was banging that girl on a table, and he can prove it, then I'll call off the auction. A click of a button and it'll disappear." As if to demonstrate, she clicked her mouse cursor on the LIST ITEM button. The screen blanked, refreshed and the countdown started. In ten days, she'd have a buyer for her body.

"NO!" Violet reached for the mouse, but Flavia closed the browser before her hand could make contact. Violet's eyes shimmered with tears. "What have you done?"

Flavia lifted her chin. "I've taken control of the situation. The ball's in James' court now. When he confesses to his cock-up and explains to me what he was doing, I'll show him the auction. He'll see what a mess he's made, and then I'll tell him he'll have to explain to all our friends and relatives why the wedding's cancelled. I'll call off the auction, he can call off the wedding, the world will know him for the wanker he is, and we can all get on with our lives."

Violet burst out laughing. "You mean it's all a bluff? You don't intend to go through with the auction?"

Flavia cracked a smile for what felt like the first time in a week. "Shit, no. What if the guy who won was some wrinkly old man who couldn't get it up? I'd die of laughter. James has ten days to get his arse to my house so I can confront him in person."

Violet wiped away tears of what Flavia hoped was mirth. "I sure hope you know what you're doing. You keep an eye on that auction and don't let it finish, or you'll have one angry winning bidder on your hands."

Flavia nodded fervently. "Of course. I can't believe you thought I'd actually do it, Vi. I'd never sell myself. Not for any price."

SIX

"Four!"

Xan tried to ignore Jay's shouting as she checked her morning emails. Ooh, good. She had four quotes for the new advertising campaign and they were all well under her budget estimate. Better yet, three of them were available for filming during the week the resort was closed, so there wouldn't be any issues with guest privacy violations, because there wouldn't be any guests to violate. Or video. Now to decide which company to work with.

"Four!" Something thwacked into a palm tree outside her window, showering the pandanus below with orange, golf-ball-sized globes and a flailing rat.

Rats. Horrible things. Xan made a note to email Maintenance to arrange for more rat baits. The vermin bred faster than they could kill them. Bloody randy rats. Worse than rabbits.

"Four...fuck!" Something clattered on the roof. Xan caught a glimpse of something that caught the sunlight in a silvery shimmer before it fell past her window and vanished into the undergrowth.

"Bloody rock stars. Worse than rats," she grumbled as she stalked outside to investigate.

The paths around the building were fortunately free of rock stars – perhaps Jay had finished causing trouble and he'd slunk off to his house to drink himself into yet another stupor. She doubted it, though. He wasn't usually that thoughtful.

"Four!" he shouted behind her.

Xan spun, but saw nothing until she shaded her eyes and saw the idiot on the hotel roof. "Four what?" she demanded.

"Dunno," he shouted back. "Stupid golfing jargon. I guess they figure it's more polite than, 'Fucking watch out 'cause there's a speeding golf ball flying at you!'"

Xan glimpsed a flash of silver. A swish and a thwack sent a white missile off the roof and into the satellite dish.

Jay let out a whoop and did a crazy war dance on the roof. "Hole in one!"

"You can't play golf on the hotel roof!" Xan hissed. "You shouldn't even be up there. What if you break a window?"

Jay shrugged. "Then I'll have to pay for repairs. They're my windows." He lined up another shot and swung his golf club.

The ball arced off the roof and plopped into the water beside the jetty.

Jay swore.

Another ball sailed across the jungle. It hit the satellite dish with a sharp crack, taking a bite out of it.

"Damn it, Jay, stop doing that! No playing golf at the resort! If you want to play golf, fly out to the golf course on the mainland!"

Like he listened. Jay leaned over, grabbed a handful of balls and lined them up along the roof. "I like playing with my balls right here. Whatcha going to do about it, Zzzan?" he drawled, lifting his club.

Thwack.

Thwack.

Thunk.

"Fuck." Jay stomped across the roof to retrieve his lost club, but after peering over the edge for a moment, decided he didn't need it and pulled another out of his golf bag.

"Mr Felix! Mr Felix!" Cam and Seb from IT tumbled out of the foyer door in the world's nerdiest circus act.

Jay lowered his club. "What?"

"If you break the satellite dish, it'll be weeks before we can get it repaired."

Jay shrugged. "So make the call to the repair guy. I'll make my own entertainment." He lined up another shot.

"There'll be no adult movies and no internet!"

The golf club clunked to the roof. "What do you mean?" Jay demanded.

"If you break that, there'll be no TV channels at the hotel and no internet access at all. Not for weeks." Seb dropped to his knees. "Please, Mr Felix. Don't do it!"

Cam glanced at Xan before adding his plea: "All the hotel guests will complain if they can't get their channels. We'll be buried in complaints calls. We won't get any work done because all we'll be doing is answering the phone."

Xan snorted. These two might be good with computers, but she didn't believe either of them cared about complaints calls. No, it was the downed channels and lack of internet that had them both desperate to stop him.

"Can't miss the *Simpsons*," Jay said, stowing his golf club back in the bag. He jerked his chin at the satellite dish. "I hit it a couple of times already. Is it still okay?"

A battered golf bag rolled off the roof and into shrubbery. Jay wrapped his legs around a palm tree that topped the roof. To Xan's horrified fascination, he slid down the trunk, landing with a thump on the sand. Dusting off his hands, he said, "We should go check."

The two geeks followed Jay at what Xan figured was a respectful distance to the fenced communications compound. Not that a security gate would stop any of them – one swipe of Jay's wrist and the lock unlatched with an audible click. Xan reached the compound just in time to hear Jay ask, "So, did I break it?"

"I dunno," Cam said. "Only way I can tell is by checking the connections on a TV or a computer. If I can't get them to work, then it's time to get the repair guy in because only he knows how to fix this. We'll have to call him."

Jay shrugged. "Let's go watch some TV, then."

All three of them trooped back into the building while Xan tagged along, figuring that the manager needed to know whether communications were down because of the idiot owner or not.

Seb grabbed the remote and turned on the tiny LED TV in the corner of the IT office. Nobody breathed while the loading screen appeared, then the list of available channels.

Glancing at Xan, Seb deliberately skipped over the adult movie channels to pick one that showed news instead.

Good call, Xan reflected. If she had to watch some silicone-enhanced, spray-tanned porn star getting more action than she was, she'd go back outside and smash the satellite dish herself.

"…And just when we thought we'd seen the end of that failed brothel registration bill, an independent senator has vowed to bring in his own bill, outlawing prostitution in Western Australia. This extraordinary pronouncement comes after an Australian girl, calling herself Miss Chastity, chose to auction her virginity online. There's been a massive social media outcry. Some calling her a whore, others proclaiming their support for a girl who wants to get ahead. The price of purity? The auction has only been open for less than a day and the bidding's almost up to half a million dollars. Senator Sinclair says that there should be laws to prevent the auction from going ahead, or other girls may get the same idea. We cross live now to Senator – "

"God, turn it off," Xan blurted out. She felt sorry for Aussies who'd voted in the recent elections. The politicians they knew had been such a pack of jokers that they'd voted for anyone else to get the idiots out of office. The result had been a bunch of crazies that fought like cats in parliament. Senator Sinclair was one of the more conservative ones, but that didn't mean she wanted to listen to him.

Mercifully, the screen went black.

"Looks like the uplink's still all right," Cam announced happily.

Xan crossed the room to take a look at the man's

monitor. Why wasn't she surprised? The screen showed the search results for...AUSTRALIAN VIRGINITY AUCTION. Plenty of text and a plethora of pictures, all showing the same bikini-clad body, minus the girl's head. Men were all alike – show a bit of skin, suggest sex, and you had their undivided attention.

"Right. If everything's all right then, I'll head back to my office," Xan said, striding out.

As her heels ticked across the tiles, Xan's thoughts strayed to the girl auctioning herself. She wasn't sure whether to feel sorry for the girl or applaud her. On the one hand, she was selling her body...but on the other, she was selling her body for her own benefit. One night as a prostitute and she'd have enough money to buy a house. Or not work for ten years.

One thing was certain: Xan wasn't the only one missing out on action. Miss Chastity evidently had, too. Idly, Xan wondered if there were any books in the hotel library about virginity auctions. Given the number of romance and erotica books in there, there had to be at least one. Hadn't Annette been talking about one at breakfast a few weeks back? She hoped it ended well, unlike Jay's last not-really-a-relationship.

Xan decided to detour through the library on her way back to her office. She needed something new to read.

<h1 style="text-align:center">SEVEN</h1>

"So what do you think? Plum or pink?" Flavia held up the lipsticks.

Violet was so fixated on her phone, she didn't respond.

Huffing in annoyance, Flavia snatched the phone. "What are you reading? The latest pictures of someone's lunch can't be that important."

Violet bit her lip. "Have you been checking the auction? Do you know how much money people are willing to pay for one night with you?"

"Shh!" Flavia glanced around, but no one looked like they were listening. "You're the only person I've told. No one but us and James ever needs to know about this."

Violet pinned her with a sceptical stare. "Does James know yet?"

Flavia squirmed. "No. Last weekend he had to work both days and this weekend he says he's too busy to drive up, too."

"What about you and your car? Have you forgotten how to drive?"

Flavia dropped her gaze to her thong-clad feet. "No. It's just that I don't want to tell him in front of his housemates or the guys he works with. I get enough whistles and catcalls as it is. I swear Doug only talks to my boobs or my bum – he wouldn't recognise my face, because he's never looked at it. If he knew I'd put my body up for auction to the highest bidder…God, no."

"He couldn't afford you. Nobody could. Have you seen the bidding?" Violet persisted.

Flavia shook her head. "It doesn't matter. Not like I'll go through with it anyway. You couldn't pay me enough to – "

"A million dollars? Would you do it for a million dollars?"

Flavia snorted. "Nobody would pay that much for me."

"Not yet, but near enough. Look if you don't believe me." Violet grabbed her phone and swiped the screen into life. "There. At last bid, they're offering you one pay check short of a million and the auction still has three days left to go. Honey, you have to go see him. Call this whole thing off before it's too late."

Flavia felt sick. She'd have to be crazy to turn down that kind of money. "What if I don't?"

"Don't see him, or don't call it off?" Violet held up her hands. "Wait, don't answer that. If you have to ask, you're not thinking straight. Get in the car. I'm driving you to Midland. We'll go to the garage where James works. You'll take him aside and talk to him. If I have to chain you both to the petrol pumps until you talk to each other, we're going to get this mess sorted today."

For a moment, Flavia tensed for a fight, but the tiny voice in her head that she'd been ignoring for a week piped up that Violet had a point. The sooner James called off the wedding, the better. She relaxed. "You're right."

"Of course I am."

For a forty minute drive, it felt far too short. All too soon, Violet pulled up outside the garage.

Flavia took several deep breaths before she exited the car. Striding across the concrete, she held her head high. She wasn't in the wrong here. He'd betrayed her and he'd bloody well pay for it.

At the reception desk, she asked for James. The spotty sixteen-year-old at the desk nodded and skittered out to the workshop in search of him.

Flavia eyed the chairs in the waiting room with longing. She wanted nothing more than to sink into one of them and out of sight, so she could hide from the coming confrontation.

"My hot little Vee! What a surprise!"

Flavia winced at the line from the sordid video. She was no one's hot little Vee, not any more. Especially not his.

"I'd kiss you, baby, but I'm covered in oil. Two guys called in sick today, so I'm stuck doing routine services and oil changes. Why the surprise visit?" James' jaunty grin was the only bit of him that wasn't covered in grease. Even his hair was slick with the stuff.

Flavia felt ill. "Can I talk to you a minute? In private?"

Spotty Boy's face fell.

Flavia led the way outside. James' shuffling footsteps followed her out to the edge of the forecourt, where the sound of passing traffic should muffle their conversation from the garage full of eavesdroppers.

"What is it, baby? You getting nervous about the wedding and what comes after?"

The horrible picture of James pounding that prostitute flashed into the forefront of her mind. Flavia nearly gagged. "Yes. No. I mean, it's off. The wedding's off, James. I can't marry you."

The dickhead laughed. "You are scared, aren't you, baby? Don't worry – we'll make the first time real quick. Sex is nothing to be scared of. It's fucking awesome. You'll see."

"How would you know?" she demanded.

He didn't even blink. "Everyone knows sex is fun. It'll be just like jacking off, only better."

Flavia wanted to wipe the grin off his face with a sander. Scraping away skin and muscle and…

"Like it was at Davo's buck's night last week?" she bit out.

His eyes widened slightly. "Davo? Nah, that was a pub crawl. I don't remember much of it. I was too sick, remember?"

Sick was right, but not in the way he meant it. "Someone videoed it, James. There's a video on the internet of you with…another girl." She couldn't bring herself to say she knew the girl was a hooker.

"Not me, baby. You know you're the only one I love." The lie tripped off his tongue, followed up by a boyish grin that made him look like a bloody angel. Devil, more like.

"Watch the video, James. Ask Davo about it. He knows." Flavia drew in a deep breath. "It's over, James. The wedding's off. You've ruined everything. And you know what? You can call all the guests and tell them. Tell them why we won't be getting married."

"Baby, be reasonable. I don't even remember what happened that night," James began. "You're just overreacting. Must be that time of the month or cold feet or you just getting scared of losing your v-card. When you calm down, we'll talk about this again."

Flavia opened her mouth to shout at him.

James held up his hands. "Ah-ah-ah, no more getting hysterical. Call me when you calm down and want to apologise for even considering cancelling the wedding." He winked. "You know how to make it all right, baby. But not right now – I have a couple more cars to service before you can service me with that sexy mouth of yours. Go shopping with your friend over there and come back when you're ready to be reasonable."

Before Flavia could stop spluttering in fury, James broke into a jog, gave her a jaunty wave, and disappeared into the garage.

Flavia stormed back to Violet's car and slammed the door behind her.

"How'd it go?" Violet chirped.

"He wants me to go shopping with you, rethink things, then come back and apologise, before giving him a blowjob."

"He...WHAT?"

Flavia chewed her lip. "Let's go shopping and buy some knives. Then we'll come back and when he whips his dick out..."

Violet snorted. "No, that'll land you in prison, too. You can't cut his dick off. Though if you're lucky, he'll catch something horrible from that prostitute and it'll fall off all by itself." She wet her lips. "The million dollar auction man isn't looking so bad at the moment, is he?"

Flavia whipped out her phone and sent James a text message, telling him to call all the wedding guests to cancel the wedding. She wouldn't contact him again until he'd done it.

"I'm not selling myself short, Vi," she vowed. "Not to James or any other man who pays for sex. I'm worth more than that, surely!"

"Mm-hmm," Vi said vaguely as she pulled out into traffic.

For all her brave words, the tiny voice in the back of Flavia's mind taunted her that if James no longer wanted her, who would?

Some crazy man who was willing to pay a million dollars for one night with her, she reminded herself. Even if she'd never sell herself, it was a comforting thought she was worth a million dollars.

EIGHT

Was she imagining it, or did Jay look a little less crazy today? Xan eyed him from the other side of the pub, wondering whether she should approach him or just leave him to his drinking. He'd fall off his bar stool soon enough without any help from her.

She squinted at the drink in front of him and was surprised to see that he had a beer and not his usual bourbon bottle. Maybe he really was starting to get over Phuong. If he wasn't drunk yet, then she should risk speaking to him now instead of later.

Weaving between tables and potted palms, Xan made her way through the jungle to the bar. Magic Marcel was on duty tonight and, true to his name, he produced her favourite drink as if he'd read her thoughts and conjured it into being. The iced ginger beer slid down her throat, leaving behind the faint but familiar burn of alcohol.. Or was it the ginger that left her lips tingling? It didn't matter. The local beer was one of the more blissful bits about working in Broome.

Jay…was a blight on her whole bloody day. She'd avoided him for as long as she could, but she knew she had to tell him. If she got it over with, she could enjoy her beer and the rest of her evening in peace.

Sighing, Xan carried her drink to his table. He nodded in way of greeting and continued drinking. He might not be into the bourbon tonight, but that didn't make him any less of an alcoholic.

"I've booked an advertising company to help raise the resort's profile in the media. A film crew will be here the week we're closed to guests, so they'll be able to take footage of whatever they like. I have two airlines already interested in showing the video to all their Australian passengers, and I'm waiting to hear back from three more. By Friday, I – "

"Fuck, do you ever stop working? It's after five. Knock off already. I have." Jay took a deep draught of his beer.

Xan frowned. "I thought you might like to know what I'm doing to keep your business in profit. Sorry for thinking you might give a shit." She seized her drink and marched across the pub to a table as far from the wanker as possible. Slumping into a chair, she checked to make sure the pot plant jungle hid her from his sight before she pulled out her book. Now she'd told him about the film crew, she had finished work for the day. She could relax and live in a romantic fantasy world that could only exist between the pages of a book, because all real men were bastards.

"Good girl." A glass clunked on her table and Xan

looked up to meet Jay's approving expression. "Is it any good?" He jerked his chin at the book.

"What do you care?" Xan said, snapping it shut. "I'm off duty, which means I don't have to deal with your shit. Go away. Go bother someone else."

"I want to know your opinion. I figure you'll be more honest than most, because you don't care what I think about you." He pushed the glass across the table. "I even brought a peace offering."

"What's in it?" She peered suspiciously into the drink. "If you're trying to drug me…"

Jay snorted. "No idea what's in it. Ask the barman. He made it. He says he knows what you like because you always order the same thing."

Iced ginger beer. Xan sniffed the glass delicately, then folded her hands in front of her on the table. "Just hurry up and ask your question, so I can go back to my book."

"That good, huh?" Jay grabbed the paperback and flicked through the pages.

While she waited for him to lose interest in a book that he couldn't possibly like, Xan drained the last of her drink. The beer Jay had brought fizzed seductively, the bubbles winking at her through the glass.

"So you think a girl selling her virginity is a good thing?"

Xan almost spat out her drink, but she managed to control herself. Just barely. "What?"

"That chick on TV. Now you're reading a book about a girl auctioning herself off to the highest bidder. You think it's a good idea?"

"It's her body. Her choice." Even as she said the words, they sounded hollow.

Jay wouldn't let it drop. "Would you do it?"

"Bloody hell, no!" Xan let out a shaky laugh. "Even if I did have my virginity to sell. Did you see how much money that auction's up to now? The only men who have that kind of money are rich, old businessmen who'd have to use Viagra to do the deed. Ugh. Dirty old men in expensive suits, except they'd be out of the suits and…oh, I don't want to think about it."

"Double standards, Xan. You think what the girl's doing is fine, but the bloke who helps her do it is a dirty old man by default." For the first time, Xan thought Jason looked angry. "What if he's not old?"

Xan's gaze strayed to the book Jay still held in his hands. "Well, if he was someone she knew, or someone she might normally have a relationship with, without having to be paid for it, or someone she actually wanted…" She trailed off, then added, "It's the money. Men who pay for sex evidently can't get it any other way."

"What if he's not paying for the sex? What if he's only paying the money so he knows he'll be her first? He'd be saving her from all the dirty old men, making sure her first time is memorable, all the while knowing that she wouldn't have any one to compare him to. No prior expectations. Just…eager to experience something new and he'd get to share that with her." The dreamy look in his eyes told Xan Jay believed every word of the tale he spun. Who was he spinning it for – her or himself? "Don't you wish someone had made your first time perfect, Xan? Don't you think that's what the auction girl's really after – someone to make her feel like she's wanted and valued?"

Xan rose. "I think I've had enough to drink and it's time

for me to go start dinner." She hurried out of the bar before he could follow her. Not that it mattered – he knew where she lived. Maybe she should eat in the staff dining room tonight. The food wasn't that bad, and it had the added bonus that Jay never set foot inside the place.

When she reached the path outside without hearing any following footsteps, she slowed down. She'd never tell him, but Jay was right about one thing: a girl did want to feel her first time was special, because it wasn't something you forgot. She truly hoped the auction girl got exactly what Jay had described – a man who'd make her first time all that and more – instead of some rich bastard who made her feel cheap even as he paid her a million dollars. If only life were like a romance novel. Then she'd know for sure that the girl would get a happy ending.

Speaking of happy endings and romance novels – where was hers? Xan cursed, realising she'd left it in the bar. If she sneaked back in, maybe she'd be able to retrieve her book without Jay noticing her. Maybe…

Xan retraced her steps and peered through the potted palms, scanning the pub patrons for Jay's unmistakeable figure. Huh. He must have left, stumbling out into the dark to pass out under a palm tree again. That'd make retrieving her book so much easier, even if it did mean more trouble tomorrow morning.

As Xan approached her table, she realised that the surface gleamed like it had just been cleaned. No empty glasses or books in sight. Sighing, she headed for the bar. "Marcel? Did you pick up the book I left on the table?"

Marcel finished pulling a beer and set the pint glass on a tray already half-full of drinks, ready to serve. "No, Mr Felix took it. He said he'd give it back to you."

Wonderful. So Jay was probably going to pass out on her veranda or in her office. Thank God for Housekeeping, or she'd have to clean up the mess herself.

Unless she kicked him off the veranda while he was still conscious…

Xan thanked Marcel and headed home. She managed a smile and a nod for everyone she passed on the darkened path, but she didn't stop to chat.

Don't let there be a drunk rock star on the doormat. Don't let there be a drunken rock star on the doormat. Oh please, don't let there be…

She breathed a sigh of relief as she surveyed her rock-star-free deck. Unfortunately, her book wasn't waiting for her, either.

Bloody Jay. Happy endings would have to wait until someone found him and her book in the morning. Once again, her happiness depended on a man with a reputation for making a bloody mess of things. Wasn't that just the story of her life?

NINE

You have less than ten minutes to call me, you rat bastard, Flavia thought, eyeing the auction countdown timer. Now, less than nine.

Her phone sat on the desk beside her, tempting her to pick it up and call James so she could tell him how much other men thought she was worth. The online news sites had been calling her the Million Dollar Girl for a week now, since the bidding hit seven figures. It hadn't stopped there, though there'd been no new bids in the last two days. Social media had worse names for her, but they didn't know her real name, so it didn't matter. The red numbers stood out against the stark, white background, telling the world she was worth a fortune to…someone.

But not James.

They'd been so perfect for each other. Since forever. He'd been her first crush, her first kiss, her first date, her first…everything. Now, he'd be the first man to break her heart.

As the seconds ticked away and her phone maintained its stubborn silence, a splash of water landed on her keyboard, followed by another. Shit, she wasn't crying over that waste of space, was she?

Flavia swiped the tears from her eyes and stared at the screen. Now only six minutes to go.

She had to be crazy to do this. Crazy to give up on the man she loved, the wedding she wanted, and sell herself to the highest bidder. She'd proved her point, hadn't she? Men thought she was worth spending a million dollars.

And James had thrown all that away with one thrust of his hips…

She'd be crazy to go back to him, knowing he'd cheated on her. What kind of low-life paid for sex?

Her phone rang and she snatched it up. "Hello?" Hope blossomed in Flavia's breast.

"Why haven't you cancelled the auction yet?" Violet demanded.

Hope died. "I will. I'm just…waiting for James to call so I can tell him about it."

"You mean you haven't told him? I thought that was the whole point of this ridonkulous revenge thing you've got going on here." Violet sighed heavily. "Just cancel the crazy thing, will you?"

"Fine." Flavia stabbed the mouse button, telling the website to end her auction. For a moment, the screen froze, then reloaded with a pop-up congratulating her on selling her item – to someone called Lucky Jason, who it told her it had already notified about his winning bid. "Fuck!"

"What is it?"

"I told it to end the auction, so it ended it early and sent a message to the highest bidder!"

Violet burst out laughing. "You're so full of shit, V. I believed you for a moment there."

"Well, you better believe it, because I'm not joking. Oh fuck, what am I going to do now?"

"You have two choices. You can tell the guy you only made the auction as revenge on your boyfriend and get blacklisted forever, or you can go ahead and act like the whole thing's legit and you're going to go through with it. Get him to send you a photo and a police clearance and evidence that he has the money for cash on delivery, like you said in the description. Give him a crazy deadline, like 48 hours. I bet he can't give you all three of them. Police clearances take a couple of weeks."

Flavia breathed again. "All right, I will. I'll see you tomorrow, right?"

"Sure."

They said their goodbyes and ended the call.

Somebody had won the auction to pay for a night with her. Flavia's stomach roiled. Sex with a stranger. Oh God, what if she couldn't find a way out of it? What if she had to get naked, let him touch her, let him…

She bolted for the toilet just in time to bring up her lunch. She stayed crouched over the toilet bowl, thankful that the rest of her family were out for the day, until she was sure her heaving stomach had nothing left to vomit up. Rinsing her mouth in the bathroom, Flavia eyed herself in the mirror. She didn't look like a prostitute. She looked like a travel agent. The trustworthy sort of girl people wanted to book their flights, tours, accommodation and travel insurance, and be at the other end of the phone to soothe them if something went wrong.

Flavia drew in a deep, calming breath…or at least it was supposed to be calming. She grabbed a dozen more, in the hope that together they'd have the required effect.

She had to email the buyer and tell him that the deal was off. Due to circumstances beyond our control, that particular experience was cancelled. Perhaps sir would like to book a city tour or a massage at the day spa instead?

Hysterical laughter bubbled up in her throat. A man who was willing to pay a million dollars for sex probably had his own chauffeur and masseuse.

As Flavia sat down at the desk again, trying to compose herself, her phone beeped to indicate an incoming message.

She threw the phone on the desk and opened the email on the computer instead.

Dear Miss Chastity, she read.

In anticipation of winning the auction, I had these prepared for you in advance. Please find attached a photograph of me, a screenshot of one of my Swiss bank accounts, a copy of a current police clearance, and details of a booking at a suitable hotel, as well as a flexible flight booking to the nearest airport. If you let me know the date and time of your flight, I will arrange for you to be met at the airport and transferred to the hotel.

This time I really think I am,

Lucky Jason

She moved the cursor to reply to his email, but her curiosity won. How had he managed to get a police clearance so fast when it normally took weeks? Maybe it was fake. Flavia clicked on the first attachment.

Dated the same day as his first auction bid, it looked like Jason had arranged the clearance not long after bidding. And there in police-watermarked printout, it said he'd never been convicted of a crime.

Just because he wasn't a criminal didn't mean he wasn't dangerous. Lots of men weren't criminals. Maybe the answer to why he had to pay for sex was in the photo he'd sent.

Wetting her lips, Flavia opened the picture. And laughed.

Jason had sent her a magazine centrefold of...sheer, naked, masculine perfection. His man bits were screened by a well-placed guitar, but it was clear the model didn't care he was lolling naked on a beach. Flavia's eyes caressed the lines of hard muscle up to his face...and recognised the man. Not a model — a rock star. He'd sent her a centrefold of Jay Felix, the rock star every girl in Australia...no, the world...had a crush on.

Jay Felix the rock star, darling of millions, having to pay for sex? In whose dreams?

She flicked through the rest of the documents — flight and hotel bookings for Broome — before the name of the hotel caught her eye: Romance Island Resort.

That was the celebrity place, wasn't it? The exclusive resort that everyone going to Broome asked about, but the astronomical prices were too high for any normal person to pay. She'd seen the brochure picture often enough to know it looked like absolute paradise, with the pristine white beaches fringed in palm trees, enticing you to come and try the jewel-coloured waters.

If you could afford to swim in an ocean of sapphires and topaz…

For a wild moment, Flavia toyed with the idea of accepting the travel arrangements, only to claim breach of contract when she met the man, as he wasn't Jay Felix and didn't look a thing like him.

What was the man's name again?

Flavia clicked on the police document again and this time, she paid attention to the details. Mr Jason Kendrick Felix, listed as living at a Sydney address, born 20 June…

She didn't hesitate. Clicking open her web browser, Flavia searched for more information on Mr J K Felix.

Ten minutes later, she laid down her pen and surveyed her hastily scribbled notes. Mr Jason Kendrick Felix, known by his stage name of Jay Felix, was the lead singer of Chaya until they broke up a few months ago. He was indeed born on the 20 June and he owned properties in Sydney, Gold Coast and Broome. A hotel in Broome, to be precise – the very Romance Island Resort everyone wanted to stay at. One of the more rabid fan sites offered to give out a phone number – for a price – that fans desperate to meet their idol could contact to apply to work as his personal assistant. The ad implied that the assistance required would be very personal and quoted some of their happy customers. Flavia's personal favourite was:

"OMG OMG OMG!!!!!!!!! 1NITE SEX ON BEACH

WITH JAY!!! AMAZEBALLS!!!!!" This stunning statement was credited to a user who called herself Jayz Cox Sok.

Flavia didn't know whether to laugh or cry. Maybe a bit of both. She couldn't deny she'd often wondered what it would be like to get up close and personal with the hot rock star…maybe even fantasised about it once or twice in high school…but to go work for him, take his money, just for the chance to sleep with him? It smacked of desperation she didn't understand.

Was that why Jay had wanted to buy her virginity? Did he want her as his extremely personal assistant? Personal assistants took care of travel arrangements, appointments and all the tiny details that made life go smoothly for their high-powered executive clients. Much like a good travel agent did. Except bidding on a virginity auction implied…no, screamed at the top of its lungs that he wanted his personal assistant to gratify his sexual whims, too.

He'd seen her headless photo, so he knew whether her body appealed to him…but did he know what her job was, too? Had he somehow stumbled on her identity and all her efforts at anonymity were shot to shit?

What if her boss found out about the auction? Or her family? What if he let slip during one of his press interviews that he'd won the virginity auction and revealed her identity to the entire world media?

Oh God. A rock star had bought her virginity. She'd never be able to show her face in public again.

TEN

Xan breathed a sigh of relief. She'd managed to persuade all the staff except six essential personnel to take time off at Easter, when the resort was closed. Just her, the two IT guys, Jackie from Housekeeping, Lee from Maintenance and a chef whose name she could never remember. Peter? Patel? Something beginning with P, anyway. She'd considered not approving the IT guys' application to stay at the island during the shutdown, but they'd insisted on the need to install some long-overdue upgrades to the operating system. After several minutes of listening to their spiel on bugs, fixes and a whole lot of technical gibberish that made her tune right out, she gave in just so that they'd stop talking. It was probably best to have some IT staff on the island. After all, if the film crew got into technical difficulties downloading the day's footage, she didn't want to be trying to do tech support. Let the IT guys handle it.

A chiselled chest caught her eye, moving down the beach, and Xan cursed. Not six people – seven. If rock stars counted as people. Maybe if she hurried, she could catch up to him and persuade him to leave the island for Easter so she could breathe easily about the film crew. If he passed out drunk in one of the public areas, she'd need more than Jackie and Lee to clean up the mess before the video crew stumbled upon it. On him, more like – he'd be right in the middle of the mess. She'd babysat better behaved toddlers.

"Jay!" she shouted, moving at a brisk trot along the boardwalk until her shoes sank into the sand. "Jay, I need to talk to you!"

He slowed, turned and spread his arms in an open invitation. Did he seriously expect her to hug him? Jay evidently didn't realise the geeky IT guys were more her type.

As Xan drew closer, she realised that his broad smile wasn't his usual smarmy one, with the slightly raised eyebrows and that look in his eye that said the lurking sex maniac would surface the moment he smelled desire in the water. Or the forced one he adopted when his sister, Jo, called. Instead, he looked…positively cheerful.

Let it mean that he had plans for Easter which would take him far away from here, she prayed to any deity listening.

"What are you doing for Easter?" she blurted out, crossing her fingers.

"Why? Are you planning on asking me out for a dirty weekend, Xan?" He laughed. "I never would have believed it, but to hear it from your own lips…" He had that wicked look in his eyes again, the one he got when he was teasing his sister. Like he knew he was a shit stirrer and he was just saying things to get her to explode.

"Don't be ridiculous," she snapped. For a moment, she wished he'd look hurt or something. Did nothing dent his monstrous ego? "I'm asking because the film crew will be here on Good Friday and they're filming over the weekend. I need to know you'll behave yourself and not do anything stupid while they're here. It costs a lot of money to shut the hotel down for a week of filming and I don't know when we'll be able to do it again, if at all. We can't have them here when the place is full of guests because of the hotel's reputation for privacy." She took a deep breath.

"You'll barely see me, I promise." He laughed again, as if at a private joke.

Xan turned his words over in her head. "I'll barely see you because you'll be off the island, enjoying yourself somewhere else, or I'll barely see you because you're going to pretend the island is a nudist colony so you can show off your bare arse?"

He looked smug. "Oh, my arse will be bare, all right, along with the rest of me. I'm having a friend over for the Easter weekend and we'll probably spend most of our time inside my villa. We'll be much too busy to even notice your camera crew."

"Another mail-order bride? Did you get a Russian one this time?" The words were out before Xan had thought them through, and she regretted them instantly.

Now she'd hurt him. Jay's voice was chilly and distant. "No." He started to walk away.

Xan considered doing the same, but couldn't bring herself to do it. Instead, she hurried to catch up to him.

"I'm sorry. That joke was in poor taste. I shouldn't have said it. But whoever she is, if you don't know her all that well, at least make sure you've done a security check on her first. I don't want..." Actually, she couldn't quite work out what she didn't want. Him killed? She wanted to strangle him almost daily, but she didn't want him dead.

Jay's eyes looked more human than she'd ever seen them as he stared directly at her. For a second, she could have sworn he was just a man and the rock star didn't exist. "Yeah, me neither." Xan had never heard his tone sound so soft. He lifted his chin in that peculiar way guys did instead of nodding like normal people. "I'll call the band's security consultant and get him to check her out."

Chaya had a security consultant? Or they did have. Normal bands had managers and groupies and roadies and maybe PR people, but what sort of band had a security consultant? Maybe all the big ones did and no one talked about it, Xan mused, deciding to ask Dennis from Security about it when he got back from leave. Not until after Easter, though.

Maybe when the girl arrived, she'd call the guys at Broome Police Station to run a quick check on her, too. The last thing she needed for the photo shoot was a murder scene. If Xan wasn't going to kill Jay Felix over the Easter weekend, then no one else was allowed to, either.

ELEVEN

Violet threw herself on Flavia's bed. "So, what excuses has the dirty old man come up with for why he couldn't get all your documents to you in time?"

"None. They were in my inbox within five minutes of the auction ending. Everything. Even a signed confidentiality agreement." Flavia swallowed. "And there's more. He wants a police clearance from me to make sure I'm not a murderer, he says." Her laughter sounded slightly hysterical.

Violet evidently didn't notice, because her giggling sounded sane. "Well, there's your way out. It'll take you weeks to get one and Easter's less than a week away."

Flavia shook her head. "They say that, but it only takes weeks if they have to check old records and stuff. I've lived my whole life here in York. Sergeant Ford had it ready for me in less than an hour."

"He won't know that, your would-be punter. Just point him to the police website. Weeks," Violet insisted.

"It won't work. I think he knows who I am. I think he wants me to work for him." Flavia's voice died so that the last words came out in a strangled whisper.

"You have a job. One you're good at. Why the hell would he think you want to become his permanent mistress? The auction was for one night. One time. Say you can't. Say you got drunk last night and slept with someone you met at the pub. Really get drunk and pick up some bloke at the pub." Panic widened Violet's eyes. "You can't seriously be thinking of going through with it!"

Flavia swallowed. "I checked the confidentiality agreement. The only way I can guarantee he can't talk about me is if I go through with the auction. No deal, and he can tell the world my name and where I live."

Violet shook her head. "You can't. You just…can't sleep with some wacko stalker. Some reclusive psycho who just happens to be able to afford to spend a million dollars to sleep with a virgin. Is he some sort of oil baron from the Middle East? An American business tycoon with a fetish for all sorts of kinky stuff? Or some ageing rock star souped up on Viagra because he's had so much sex his downstairs is all worn out?"

Flavia cracked a smile. "He's not any of those things, though you're close with the last one."

Violet screwed up her face in concentration, then smacked her hand against the bedhead. "You'll have an agreement about no kink, right? Make sure it says no performance enhancing drugs, or any drugs at all. No Viagra, no hard on, no worries!"

Jay Felix didn't need Viagra, or any other drug to make girls happy. Dozens of his happy bed-partners had told the media that much and more. The gory details had made Flavia blush until she couldn't take it any more, so she'd stopped searching the internet for the rock star who wanted to take her virginity. No, who wanted to pay her a premium so she'd give it to him. Would that be so bad?

"I don't think it'll be that easy, Vi," Flavia said. "Even if it is, I'll still have to show up at the hotel so we can both sign it before we…if we do it." She couldn't bring herself to describe the deed aloud.

Violet enveloped Flavia in a fierce hug. "Don't worry. You'll find a way out of this, and you'll come join us in Bali for the hen's trip turned girls' trip of your life. We'll laugh about this over cocktails at the hotel bar. Talk about happy hour. It'll be a whole happy week. You'll see."

And with that, they said their goodbyes, leaving Flavia alone with her thoughts. Which naturally turned toward the irresistible naked man lying on a beach in her inbox, who wanted to pay her a million dollars for one night. Other girls would be willing to pay him that for fifteen minutes, if the tales were true. If that picture was accurate…

Flavia slid onto her desk chair, bringing her computer back to life so she could search for images of rock god Jay Felix. Always grinning, always sexy…sometimes winking, rarely wearing a shirt and even if he did have a shirt or jacket, he wore it wide open. Chiselled abs, glistening with…well, it was hard to tell. Her first guess would be sweat, but in some of the photos it looked more like oil. Idly, she wondered how much they paid the makeup artist who got to oil him up in preparation for the shot. She could imagine a line of volunteers forming every time that shirt came off...

What would it feel like to spend a night with a man who had a body like that? A body he knew how to use to make a woman feel wanted, if his reputation as a legendary lover could be believed.

The thought hit her like one of the trucks barrelling along the highway.

Would it be such a bad thing to lose her virginity to Jay Felix?

TWELVE

At seven on the dot, Xan heard splashing. "Don't you own any pants?" she shouted.

Good thing there were no guests left at the hotel to see, what with them being officially closed for the week and all. Not like that had ever stopped him before.

Jay merely grinned and waved as he stroked his way across the lagoon on his back. Even with his bits on display, Xan couldn't take her eyes off him. What unfeeling deity wrapped the quintessential wanker in such perfect packaging?

One look and she craved bacon. The taste of salt from the sizzling hot flesh on her tongue…not the bowl of cardboard cereal currently sitting on the bench, waiting patiently for its milk.

Maybe it was time to cave to the pressure and buy herself some sex toys from one of the online shops.

Watching him every morning only made her crave company more. A battery-operated boyfriend like the American romance heroines all seemed to have. It's not like she needed any other bit of a man to satisfy her.

More splashing as Jay did a lap of breaststroke, sticking his Adonis arse in the air with every kick. She didn't need this kind of temptation right now – least of all from him.

"You know the lagoon's full of sharks," she hollered. "They like biting soft flesh."

She watched in satisfaction as he flipped from his front to his back again.

"Not mine!" he called back. "Besides, how am I supposed to get into shape and work on my tan when half of me's covered up? Got to look my best for my friend arriving this arvo."

Bloody Australian slang. "It's afternoon, you idiot!"

"Nope. Still bright and early in the morning. You're still in that see-through t-shirt you love to sleep in, watching your favourite breakfast show before you dig into your cereal. We both know you love watching me swim, Zzzzan." Jay laughed as he swam out of sight.

Xan's hands balled into fists, ready to smack him. He could see her shirt from that far away? Hang on, see through her shirt? Shit. She'd better wear a darker shirt tomorrow morning, then. How many mornings while she'd been perving on him had he been laughing at her boobs? Bloody rock star. He was a plague on this otherwise perfect island. A blight. A curse. A…

She watched him rise from the water, still stark naked, and walk past her window. He waved jauntily before heading into the jungle, his arse swinging with every step.

Stop looking. Stop looking at him, damn it! That's what he wants!

A clump of pandanus hid him from sight, bringing Xan back to her senses. Breakfast. Then she had a whole day of work ahead of her before she could knock off for the rest of the long weekend. She couldn't forget the film crew, either – their flight would arrive just after lunch.

The approaching storm would be gone by tomorrow morning, revealing blue skies over the picture-perfect paradise that was Romance Island Resort.

That brought the smile back to Xan's face. Even with the odd rock star rat, she still had the best job in the world.

THIRTEEN

"You take care of yourself in the city tonight. Don't you back down on a single one of the conditions we wrote into the contract. The lecherous old man will call off the deal and all this will be over. Get the hell out of there and call me the minute you arrive at Denpasar Airport, all right?" Violet enveloped Flavia in a fierce hug. "Promise?"

Flavia forced a smile as she nodded. Part of her wanted to tell Violet that she wasn't going to a city hotel to meet some old man at all, but meeting her would-be…deflowerer? Was that even a word? Whatever he was, she'd meet Jay or the man pretending to be him at Romance Island after landing at Broome Airport in a few hours' time. This whole mess might be over and done with before Violet and the other girls' plane landed in Bali.

It had to be. If Flavia had one more sleepless night like the last few, she'd go certifiably crazy. If she hadn't already.

Jay Felix, with his far-too-perfect body, had invaded her dreams and a large proportion of her waking thoughts, too. She didn't dare tell Violet that she'd considered going through with the deal, conditions or not. Or that most of the conditions were a list of all the things she'd already done with James. Well, not the kinky stuff, obviously, but anything up to actual sex. She was a virgin, not a nun. And she suspected Jay would be a million times better than James at making her heart race. She only had to close her eyes and she could almost feel Jay's hands on her, sending her soaring to undreamed-of heights.

Violet didn't seem to notice her distraction. "Au revoir, then!" And with a wave, she vanished through the departure gate.

Flavia waited a few seconds until she was certain Violet was out of sight before she headed outside. Instead of taking a taxi to the city, she wheeled her case over to the shuttle that transported passengers between the international and domestic terminals. Oh, she had a whole suitcase of clothes in the boot of her car for Bali, but that could stay there until tomorrow. She wouldn't need any more clothes except the change in her overnight bag where she was going.

If she needed clothes at all.

A vision of having sex on the beach with Jay as the sun set over the tropical ocean made her feel all warm inside. At least until she realised that the shuttle driver was shouting at her that they'd reached the terminal. Blushing furiously, Flavia stumbled off the bus. It wasn't until she reached the terminal doors that she realised she'd been dragging her case along the side without wheels. She quickly flipped it around, hoping no one had noticed. Anyone would think this was her first time on a plane. She was a travel agent, for God's sake. A professional who knew the travel industry inside out.

Throwing her shoulders back, Flavia marched through the automatic doors and joined the check-in queue. Whatever her evening held, she'd face it head-on like the professional she was. A travel agent and not a sex worker, she reminded herself.

Her boarding pass told her she had the window seat she'd requested, bringing a smile to her face. Her case was small enough to qualify as carry-on luggage, so she strode past the luggage drop-off counters with a scornful glance at all the tourists who packed way too much. One man had so many cases they threatened to fall off his luggage trolley.

"Watch out!"

The warning came too late. Flavia tripped over the wheels of a second overloaded trolley and flew forward to prostrate herself on the airport carpet.

"Are you okay?"

Flavia jumped to her feet, smoothing her dress and hoping she hadn't flashed her knickers to the whole airport terminal. "Fine. I'm fine," she snapped at the man who didn't look much older than she was.

"You should watch where you're going," he said, shoving his trip-hazard trolley closer to the luggage scales.

"So should you." Without another word, Flavia tilted her suitcase and set off for the departure lounge, biting back the names she wanted to call the overpacked idiot. She hoped the airline charged him a fortune for the excess baggage and lost half of it in transit. No one needed that much stuff for a holiday.

She sailed through security with no problems, dodging between the minesite staff taking off belts, shoes and watches to make it through the metal detectors without beeping. There was a slight delay when the security officer decided to check her for explosives, but Flavia gritted her teeth and endured the vacuuming of her shoulder and bag before the bored guard gave her the all clear. Finally. Flavia ascended the escalator to the departure lounge and surveyed the sea of fluorescent yellow and orange. It was evidently shift change day at many of the mines. She'd heard about this, but it was different to be one of the drab passengers caught in the crush of high visibility site uniforms. She'd never thought a simple grey dress could stand out so much.

Oh well. So much for blending in. Flavia found her gate and threw herself into one of the plastic seats. Air hissed out of the thin vinyl cushion beneath her in a sigh she felt like echoing. To distract her from the upcoming ordeal when she landed, Flavia flipped to a random game on her phone that quickly absorbed her attention.

The calming sequence of matching, moving and making pieces disappear occupied her so completely that the boarding call for her flight took her by surprise. Flavia stared at the time displayed on her phone – yes, she'd been sitting there for almost an hour while her butt cheeks grew numb against the unforgiving plastic. She wanted to rub the circulation back into them, but she was hardly going to do that in front of a terminal full of men. Instead, she tried to ignore the tingling as she joined yet another queue.

"Enjoy your flight," the flight attendant said as she passed Flavia her scanned boarding pass.

With a nod, Flavia moved down the aerobridge, hearing the sibilant hiss of her case wheels on the carpet as the sounds of a thousand conversations in the terminal faded. Another smiling attendant pointed out her seat and Flavia trundled her case to her place for the next couple of hours. With her phone switched off and her case in the overhead compartment, Flavia drummed her fingers on the armrest, already bored and wishing she could start watching the inflight movie early. This plane didn't have screens on the seat backs, so it must be one of those old ones with ceiling screens that descended when the flight crew decided it was time. Wonderful.

Flavia grabbed the inflight magazine and started flipping through the pages.

A night of spectacular sex or should she call off the deal?

She wanted Jay. All those pictures on the internet, invading her dreams. Even her fantasies featured him this week. If the rumours were right and he truly was the legendary lover his fans claimed him to be, one night would never be enough. She'd want more. Not just one episode, but the whole damn season. And the next, and the one after that...

She should call off the deal. Tell him she'd changed her mind.

Or she could have one night with a rock star. Enough to fuel erotic dreams for the rest of her life. And the money to travel wherever she wanted for a couple of years.

The deal didn't look so bad viewed from that angle.

Flavia scrubbed her hands across her face, trying to blot out the image of her twined around Jay's luscious body, all hard muscle and gleaming…

"We meet again."

Flavia glanced up and met the eyes of her trolley assailant. She pressed her lips together, sending up a fervent prayer that he'd go away.

"And we're seat mates. Isn't that great?"

Her eyes told him to die, but he ignored her as he shoved his bags in the overhead locker before sliding into the seat beside her. "I'm Tim." He stuck his hand out for her to shake.

Flavia felt an overwhelming urge to bite his hand. Hard. Instead, she managed a polite handshake as she told him her name. Damn all her good manners.

"You going to Broome on business?" he asked.

The sex trade. Lucrative business like you wouldn't believe. Flavia coughed, then cleared her throat to cover the hysterical laughter that threatened to escape. "Um, no. Just visiting a friend."

"You're all dressed up for your friend. Boyfriend, I take it?"

"No!" Too late, Flavia tried to cover up her slip. "Just a friend. I want to make a good impression, is all."

Tim grinned. "Online romance? You picked one hell of a tourist destination for a first date. Be careful where you sit on the beach to watch the sunset, or you'll have a hundred people taking pictures of you as you become an internet sensation. Kissing couple on Cable Beach, silhouetted against the sunset."

Flavia's blood ran cold. The video of James and his hooker had gone viral, so it had popped up in her social media feed more times than she could count, with captions like *Best Man EVER* and *Buck's Night Booty*. She never wanted that sort of fame. That's why she'd made the auction as anonymous as possible, so that by the time Jay learned her name (if he didn't already know it), he'd already signed the confidentiality agreement. "I'll keep that in mind," she said colourlessly. She paused for a moment before she recalled her manners. "Are you going to Broome for a holiday, too?"

Tim laughed so hard he shook the seat. "Hell no. This is a work trip. Me and my partner, we're filmmakers and our media company scored a contract to do some PR for one of the big Broome resorts. Filming for their new ad campaign. It's the biggest contract we've ever had, so Simmo didn't want to leave anything behind. Every camera we own, tripods, extra lenses, filters...all the cases barely fitted in the car, but he wouldn't hear of leaving it. The resort's paying for it, he said, so why not?"

Flavia's icy disapproval defrosted slightly. "And here I thought you only brought all that luggage so you could mow down unsuspecting fellow passengers."

Tim shrugged. "I said I was sorry."

Flavia couldn't recall hearing anything of the sort, but then she'd been too embarrassed and angry to want to listen to a word he said downstairs, anyway. And now she was stuck sitting next to the man for the next few hours. She imagined him as one of the difficult clients at work — perhaps one of the farmers who'd missed his flight and wanted someone to shout to about it, so all she could do was stay calm until the ordeal was over.

"Apology accepted," she said graciously, or at least that's what she was aiming for.

The flight attendant interrupted the silence to demonstrate the plane's safety features, which saved Flavia the need to say any more.

When the woman finished and her seatbelt and lifejacket were safely stowed away, Flavia ventured, "I wonder what the inflight movie will be today."

Tim surveyed the plane. "Don't think there'll be one. No screens. They usually switch them on for the safety briefing. Probably a good thing. I've seen all the decent movies out at the moment and there's none I'd want to see again. I wonder what it takes to get your film approved for release on inflight entertainment? I bet they wouldn't tell me if I asked, though."

Flavia's polite answering smile seemed to be enough to unlock the floodgates. Tim told her about his and Simmo's online video channel, the series of indie films they'd created in and around Perth, and the challenges of making it big in a world where everyone had cameras on their phones and the videos that went viral were more about being in the right place at the right time than any skill on the part of the person holding the camera. But all that would change after this job, because they'd have the money to film the first season of their series when the cheque came in.

Flavia nodded and made understanding noises as Tim gave her a blow-by-blow account of the plot of their proposed six-season series. It sounded like a mashup of every one of James' favourite TV shows, including the Aussie soap operas he watched religiously every night, though he'd deny it at the top of his voice if anyone even suggested he watched that soppy crap.

City buildings gave way to red dust, which transitioned

to ancient, weathered rock as they flew north. All too soon, clear skies gave way to stormy turbulence as clouds shrouded them.

As if to deepen the gloom, the pilot announced their approach into Broome Airport.

Flavia tightened her white-knuckled grip on the armrests as the jet bumped onto the tarmac before grinding to a halt. Hot, humid air gusted into the cabin, smelling of iron-tainted mud. Tim and the other passengers hurried out of the plane, but she took her time, dragging her bag from the locker and wheeling it slowly down the aisle. She was the last passenger off the plane, but standing at the top of the steps, she wished she'd stayed longer. The tropical air wrapped around her face like a hot plastic bag. How could anyone breathe in this humidity?

"There's air conditioning in the terminal," the flight attendant said, pointing.

Flavia clattered down the metal stairs to the tarmac, feeling the heat radiating through her shoes. She moved at a brisk trot, hoping the soles of her sandshoes wouldn't melt.

There was indeed some form of air conditioning in the terminal building, but even that struggled to push back the humidity. Or perhaps it was the crush of people, both those who had just disembarked from the plane and the families and friends who had arrived to greet them while they waited impatiently for their luggage. The baggage carriers were still unloading the plane, and taking their time, too. Working hard in this heat couldn't be fun.

Flavia wove through clumps of people, careful not to run over any toes with her bag, until she found herself outside again in a blazing sauna by herself. Bugger.

"Miss?"

She turned and met the gaze of an Asian man, who rose from his shady seat behind a potted palm tree. He definitely wasn't Jay.

"Can I help you?"

Flavia shook her head. "I'm supposed to wait for someone to pick me up."

"Then you should go back inside. That's where everyone meets, because it's cooler." He grinned.

Jay wasn't inside. Flavia was certain of that. She hadn't seen a screaming mob surrounding a man signing autographs or playing air guitar or whatever else rock stars did to work a crowd into a frenzy. No dodgy-looking blokes in hats and sunglasses, either. Well, at least not lurking by themselves. Perhaps she should go inside and look again.

"The other hotels make their drivers hold tacky signs with people's names scribbled on them. The Resort has…a different clientele. People who don't want their names up there for the general public to see." His knowing look made Flavia feel uncomfortable. How much did he know about her? The man was wearing knee socks with shorts and a button-through cotton shirt, like an overgrown schoolboy. Talk about creepy.

"Romance Island Resort?" she asked, hoping he meant some other resort. Maybe one of the expensive ones at Cable Beach.

"The very same." He eyed her. "You're my only passenger today. Is that all your luggage?"

Flavia balked. "Yes, that's all my luggage. Look, I'm here to meet Mr Felix. I'm not stupid enough to get into a car with a man I don't know who might have plans to murder me and dump my body in the desert. Unless you can give me some ID to prove you're a driver for the resort, I'm not getting into any car with you."

To Flavia's surprise, the man laughed. "I'm not a driver. I'm a helicopter pilot. And my baby is on the other side of that hangar." He pointed at a shed just inside the airport fence, then pulled out his wallet. "Here's my pilot's licence, if you don't believe me."

Flavia peered at the card. "Sho-u....Matsu-moto?" she read slowly. "What's a Japanese pilot doing in Broome?"

He laughed so hard his hands slapped his knees. "It's Shou. Like the shoe on your foot. You've never been to Broome before, have you? Japanese men built the pearling industry and most of the town here, before they were all locked up in World War II. Most of them never came back, but my grandfather's family did. I've visited relatives in Japan, but for generations of my family, like me, Broome is home. The pearls keep us here and I hope they always will."

Slowly, Flavia started to walk toward the shed. "So you're a pilot or a pearler?"

"Some women think I'm a right pearler, all right, but Mr Felix's girls have eyes for no one but him, so I'll just be your pilot today." He sounded sad.

"Girls? Mr Felix has lots of girls?" Flavia blurted out, knowing his reputation but wanting it to be wrong. She'd just be another conquest for him. An unusual and expensive one, but that's all. Her heart sank, begging her on its knees not to go through with the deal with Jay.

"I'm sure he has as many as he wants, but I've only flown two. Three if you count his sister, and four with you."

He looked like he wanted to say more, but his lips closed firmly until a helicopter came into view. "There's my baby."

He keyed in his access code on the gate and it grated open, allowing them to cross from carpark to airside. Flavia's suitcase bumped along behind her.

"You can sit in the co-pilot's seat if you like," Shou said. "Just as long as you don't touch anything. Best view in the house."

Flavia accepted his offer and climbed into the front of the bubble-like helicopter cabin. The overhead blades whirred into life so loud she could barely hear herself think. Perhaps that was a good thing. "Can you tell me about Jay's other girls?" she shouted.

Shou shook his head, tapped his headset and held out another headset to her.

She slipped it over her head and repeated her question into the tiny microphone.

"No, I can't," he said, then paused to speak to the control tower. When he was done, he added, "Romance Island Resort is special. What happens at the resort, stays at the resort. It's what the guests expect of an exclusive place like that. There's no place like it."

Flavia wasn't sure whether she felt elated or alarmed. On the one hand, if she slept with Jay, no one would ever know. On the other hand, if the man was dangerous, or not Jay at all, and she tried to back out of the deal, did that mean he could get away with hurting her? "What if something illegal happens there?"

Shou's eyes darted from his instrument display to the sky above as he lifted the helicopter into the air and started to spiral slowly upward. "Then it's reported to the hotel manager, who liaises with the police. Nothing happens on the island without Ms Lane knowing about it. If you're thinking of doing anything illegal at the resort, I recommend you don't. She knows every police officer in town and she'll send me to pick them up. You don't want to cause trouble at Romance Island Resort."

No, she didn't. Flavia felt a tiny bit safer. "What's the resort like?"

Shou leaned back in his seat, suddenly relaxed. "Romance Island is one of the most beautiful islands I've ever seen. Incredible beaches, a lagoon where you can snorkel for hours, and the sunsets…if you can, try and find a nice spot on the beach to watch every sunset and dawn, too, if you're up early enough. There's no place like it in the world." He flew over the town, the beach and through the blanketing cloud cover to clear skies. Soon all Flavia could see was ocean, red rock and vegetation desperately clawing a life out between the two.

Flavia watched it all slip past through her curved window, her thoughts seesawing between whether she should or she shouldn't.

It depended on Jay. Or the man who might or might not be Jay. God, when did this all become so complicated? She should have just gone to a pub and gone home with some bloke for the night. Wham, bam, thank you…but no, she wouldn't have done that, either.

Now, she might as well make the most of the opportunity. Whatever it held.

"There's the island, coming up now." Shou pointed.

Flavia peered at the blue heart – the lagoon Shou had mentioned – rimmed with red rock, white sand and a surprising amount of green. Buildings nestled among the trees, roofed in light green that made them blend in with their surroundings. As if the entire island was uninhabited. The only clearly visible man-made structure was a patch of paving, marked with a ringed H – the helipad.

Shou circled the island, dipping lower as he approached the landing spot. Flavia watched as a figure flew out the door of a building and pelted down the path to the helipad. A woman, she decided, as the helicopter settled on the ground. A woman who didn't look happy at all. In fact, her expression rivalled the storm clouds over town.

Shou didn't seem to notice. He grinned and waved cheerfully at her. "There's Ms Lane herself, come to greet you. You enjoy your stay, now."

Flavia cracked open the door. Meeting the hotel manager was hardly a problem, when compared to what would happen later.

FOURTEEN

The sound of the approaching helicopter alerted Xan. She was halfway out the door before she realised she still had her coffee in her hand. She set it on the unoccupied reception desk and crossed the foyer to the door. The film crew were finally here.

Yet when she reached the helipad, she couldn't see anyone but Shou with some girl in the co-pilot's seat. No sign of Simon or the other guy she'd spoken to during their video calls. Or any of the essential equipment they'd insisted on bringing and charging her for. Well, the hotel, but the hotel's budget was her responsibility and...what did it matter? Who was this girl and where were her cameramen?

When the girl reached the open gate, Xan stuck out her hand. "Xan Lane. I'm the manager of Romance Island Resort."

Xan gave the girl credit. She smiled and had a surprisingly firm handshake. "I'm here to see Mr Felix," she said.

"Are you now?"

"Yes," she said pleasantly. "If you could tell him I'm here, please."

Xan almost admired her. "What name shall I give him?"

A faint blush appeared across her cheeks. "He's expecting me."

No guest stayed at her hotel without giving suitable identification. Not even Jay's guests. "Are you a mail-order bride?" Xan demanded.

The girl's shock left her mouth hanging open. "No."

"A groupie? A fan? An ex-staff member?" Xan pressed, watching the girl's eyebrows draw down in annoyance.

"No. Not that it's any of your business, but I'm a travel agent. And I'm here as Mr Felix's guest, so unless you want me to warn my clients away from your hotel…" the girl trailed off ominously.

"So Jay's banging travel agents now?" Xan was shocked to see the girl's face flame red, but she pressed her advantage. "Did he pick you up in town on his last trip?"

"I've never met him before," the girl protested, then bit her lip.

Not a mail-order bride. Not a groupie. What did Jay need a travel agent for? He lived in a damn resort and refused to leave. A girl who hadn't met him and blushed furiously at the mention of sex. No. He couldn't be that stupid. Not even Jay would bid on that girl's virginity auction, surely.

"Follow me to Reception. I'll get you checked in and

make sure you have access to the guest facilities," Xan said, turning on her heel to head back to the hotel. She heard the girl's footsteps and trundling wheels follow her. Xan slipped behind the desk as if she processed guests every day. "Right, name?" She poised her hands over the computer keyboard. "And I'll need to see some ID, plus your police clearance."

The girl opened her mouth to argue.

Hundreds of backpackers had tried and failed. Xan cut her off before she started. "Your details are kept confidential, but we need them for legal reasons. If you go swimming in the lagoon and don't come out, we need your details to file a missing persons report with the local police. Now, ID and police clearance, or you'll have to get back into that helicopter, because you can't stay here without correct identification."

Reluctantly, the girl extracted her wallet and handed over her driver's licence. Further fossicking in her bag produced a document folder from which she pulled a crisp police clearance. "There."

"Miss Flavia…Lancaster? From York?" Xan enquired, trying not to sound gleeful. She was dying to ask the girl why she'd set up the auction, but she restrained herself. "Everything seems in order." Xan grabbed one of the VIP wristbands and set it in the scanner. "Okay, this will give you access to Jay's villa and all of the shared guest facilities. Kitchen hours are limited this week, but Jay should have the times on his room service menu. Any questions?" She passed the wristband across the counter and watched the girl…no, Flavia put it on.

Flavia shook her head. "Does Mr…does Jay know I'm here?"

Xan shrugged. "He probably heard the helicopter. I'll call him and let him know." She reached for the reception desk phone, then changed her mind. "I'll be right back." She headed for her office and closed the door before dialling the number for Villa Penguin.

"Xan. Are you finally asking me on a date?" Jay laughed.

For once, Xan had one up on him. "No. Your date for tonight just arrived, complete with her clean police clearance. Miss Chastity." She held her breath, waiting for him to confirm her suspicions. Wishing he wouldn't.

"She's here?"

Jay Felix, rock star and the biggest idiot this side of the sun, had bought a girl's virginity. Xan's already low opinion of him dropped an extra kilometre.

"Send her over!"

And have a repeat of Phuong's flight? Not bloody likely. "I'll bring her to your villa," Xan snapped. "And you'd better have clothes on this time."

"Aw, c'mon, Xan. Clothes are overrated in this heat."

Xan didn't deign to reply. Instead, she hung up and headed back to Flavia. "He knows. I'll take you to his place now."

Flavia gave a curt nod and gestured for Xan to lead the way.

Xan wondered whether the girl's confidence was faked or whether she had no qualms about selling her body to the highest bidder, whoever he might be. Did she have no conscience or doubts at all? Xan couldn't…wouldn't…ever be able to march so calmly to the house of the man she'd sold herself to. She'd been a ball of nerves on the helicopter here, and her job wasn't half as daunting as prostitution. Or first time sex.

The rain had stopped, for the moment, though steaming puddles still stood on the paths. Flavia's suitcase wheels hissed as they parted the tiny seas, all the way to Villa Penguin.

Flavia hesitated at the steps, but Xan kept going, right up to Jay's front door, which she rapped on. "Jay, your visitor's here!" Xan called through the frosted glass.

The door whirred open and Xan moved aside so that Jay could see Flavia. And so she could see them both. Flavia's eyes grew as round as her open mouth until she swallowed and seemed to get a hold of herself. Shakily, she climbed the steps, bumping her suitcase up behind her.

Jay's easy smile was already in place. So were his shorts, fortunately, though that's all he wore. Better than nothing, Xan supposed. "Come in," he said, his voice so deep he was almost purring.

Bloody tomcat, Xan thought.

"You can go now, Xan," Jay said, making shooing motions.

Xan's eyes darted to Flavia. Was it safe to leave this inexperienced girl with Romance Island's Romeo?

"Thank you. It was nice to meet you," Flavia said. Without another glance at Xan or Jay, she headed past him into the house.

Jay winked at Xan before letting the door close between them.

Xan debated whether to stick around to make sure the girl was all right, or leave before the sounds of sex started.

Listening to Jay Felix have sex with a girl he'd paid for the privilege? Ugh, no. Xan headed back to her office. Only a few hours left before her long weekend started and she was still waiting on that film crew. Where were they?

FIFTEEN

Oh God. It really was him. Jay Felix. He was hotter in person than in his pictures. Her mouth watered at the thought of running her fingers down those muscles, before pulling him hard against her for…what? Anything he wanted, she supposed.

"Come in," he said, his voice deeply emphasising the 'come'.

Flavia forgot the formidable Ms Lane. She probably forgot her own name as her feet carried her into his house. No, his hotel room, for that's what it was. A big, stark suite with hotel furnishings and nothing personal lying around, like he didn't really live here.

She stopped in the middle of the floor, wanting to sag onto the couch before her legs gave out, but if she did, she wasn't sure she'd manage to get up again. The dining table might be best. She could sit at the head of the table, place the contract documents at the other end and have the length of wood between them when he sat down to read what he could and couldn't do to her.

What he could do to her…

Flavia just made it to the table before her wobbly legs refused to hold her any more. She was in way over her head.

"Can I get you a drink?" Jay stood in the kitchen, one hand on the fridge door.

Yes, please. A glass of the strongest stuff you have, and make it a double, Flavia thought but didn't say. Instead, she quavered, "No, thank you." She stared at him and felt a blush heating her cheeks. To cover her discomfiture, she lifted her bag onto her lap and rifled through it for the folder of documents. When she found it, she held it up as a shield between her and the abs that were taunting her to taste them.

"You want to get the paperwork sorted first? Good idea. Then we're free to enjoy ourselves as much as we like." Jay moved to the table and sat on the chair closest to her, stretching his legs beneath the table until his knee bumped hers.

The contact sent a jolt that travelled right up to her heart, which did jumping jacks until it lodged in her throat as she realised that his leg remained right beside hers. Skin on skin, heating her more than she thought humanly possible.

"Mr Felix." It came out as a squeak, so she started again. "Mr Felix, I've prepared a list of acceptable conduct for you, both during and after our contract. I'm sure you were already aware of the condition that there will be no further contact between us once the transaction is complete, but there are other things that..." She watched in horror as Jay plucked the folder from her fingers and scanned the first page. He flipped to the next...and the next, until he came to the signature page. He couldn't have read them that quickly. No one read that quickly.

Jay produced a pen from his pocket and winked at her. His eyes never leaving hers, he signed the last page with a flourish and pushed the folder across the table to her. "Are we done with the boring stuff?"

Flavia stared at his signature. He'd agreed to...everything? Without even reading it? "I thought you might want to discuss..."

His finger touched her lips, effectively silencing her. "What's there to discuss? You're here because you want your first time to be with me. You tell me what you want, what you need, and I'll make sure you never forget your first time, because no one else will ever measure up." He set an envelope on top of the signed contract. "The details of a numbered Swiss account with my bid amount as the balance are in there. It's yours."

Not yet, it wasn't. First she had to...he had to... "Where would you like to do it?" Flavia choked out.

Jay chuckled. "You're eager to get my clothes off, aren't you? I figured we'd take it slowly, but it's really not up to me. When our bodies unite in shared passion for the first time and you cry out in ecstasy, everything should be just the way you like it." He leaned over the table so that his face was centimetres away from hers. "In your dreams, the wild fantasies you've woven as you wondered what it would be like with me, where did you want me to worship you?"

She was drowning in his eyes, glowing like the water of the Avon River when the sun shone just right. Drowning so deeply she'd never reach shore on her own. But in his arms…ohhhh…

"The shore," she blurted out, then added, "I mean, the beach. Ssss…sss-sex on the beach." Sand cradling her body as the warm water caressed her and Jay…he…

His leaned forward and his lips grazed hers, breaking the spell.

Flavia leaped backwards, chair and all. "No kissing! It's in the contract you just signed!"

Annoyance creased his perfect brow. "What? You can't be serious."

Flavia tried to slow her racing heart. "Read it if you don't believe me. No kissing, no kinky stuff, no – "

Jay burst out laughing. "Whatever you say, baby. How about we head out to my private beach where it'll just be you and me? Then you can decide what you want and what you don't. I'll make sure it's better than your wildest dreams."

Flavia swallowed. She believed him. And in a dream, she followed him out of the villa and onto the warm sand. Waves licked languorously at the beach, waiting for her and Jay to join them.

SIXTEEN

Xan thought she caught the sound of thumping helicopter blades, but when she walked outside to check, the sky was disappointingly clear. It was only the jet boat's throbbing engines, as Baz brought the last supply run before the weekend.

He waved from the wheelhouse and she waved back, wishing she had time to go for a spin in the Sound with him. It'd been weeks since she'd had time for a rollercoaster ride through the whirlpools, but she was dying to do it again. Soon, she promised herself. When the boat came back from dry dock next week. The freshly painted hull would slide across the surface better than the hydrofoil that belonged to one of the tour companies in town.

The tide was in, so when Baz tied up the *Argo*, he only had to heft the boxes from the deck to the jetty instead of winching them ashore. Not that he liked using it — he usually complained that the winch was too slow and he'd rather lift the boxes himself. Xan didn't mind if it was the laundry bags — those were easy to toss to the deck, no matter how low the tide. A three-metre drop didn't damage the dirty linen. But when it was a crate of milk that were all the dairy they'd have for a week, or a case of expensive spirits in glass bottles, Xan drew the line. She'd seen Baz drag the milk crates up the ladder, canted at an angle so precarious she couldn't understand how he'd managed to stop the milk bottles from tumbling into the water below.

The sound of trundling trolley wheels behind Xan told her that she wasn't the only one waiting for the supply boat — Patel and Lee headed down the jetty to collect the food so they could safely stash it in the cool room.

"Don't forget your beer, boys," Baz said, clunking a box to the boards that Xan knew wasn't on the resort's manifest.

"Remember you're both on call for the Easter weekend," she warned them.

Patel waved away her worries. "We won't forget, Ms Lane. Besides, the bar isn't open until next week. This is all the beer we have for a whole week!"

Put like that, a case wasn't likely to go very far between the two men. Xan let it go.

"No bar. But we heard the hotel bar here was one of the main attractions. Best beer in the Kimberley on tap, the website said!"

Xan whirled at the sound of an unfamiliar voice. Baz had a passenger — two, actually. Two scruffy-looking men in cargo pants and t-shirts started unloading a stack of Pelican cases that didn't look like anything the resort had ordered, either.

One of them extended a large hand. "I'm Simon and this is Tim. We spoke on the phone last week. We're here to film your island in all its glory. But without the bar, I guess."

Xan accepted the handshake, her mind trying to fill in details and coming up blank. "You were supposed to be here hours ago. I had the helicopter pilot on standby."

Tim and Simon exchanged glances. "We had so much gear, it was too much for one trip. We hired a car instead and took the boat over," Tim said loudly. Simon nodded and clambered over the seats to get another case. Tim dropped his voice to a carrying whisper, "Simmo used to work on the oil and gas rigs. Only way on and off was by helicopter. One day, the pilot was so high on drugs he decided his helicopter was a dragonfly and tried to skim across the top of the waves. A big wave washed over the top of it and Simmo and the others had to swim for their lives or sink to the bottom. Then he was stuck on a life raft with the puking pilot for two days before a survey ship picked them up. The pilot had dried out by then – no trace of the drugs in his system, so he's still licensed to fly. Simmo won't go back after that. He won't get in another helicopter, he says."

Xan nodded, though she didn't entirely believe him. Surely she'd have heard of a helicopter crash if it had almost claimed lives. She considered for a moment. Actually, she probably wouldn't. If it was the oil and gas company's helicopter, not a commercial charter, and the drilling platform was far enough offshore, it would be outside Australian jurisdiction. They wouldn't have to report the incident to anyone. It really was the edge of civilisation out here.

"Well, you're here now. I'm Xan Lane, the manager of the resort, as you've probably already guessed. We only have a skeleton staff with no guests on the island, so I've arranged to put you up in the staff accommodation. If you'll come with me, I'll get your wristbands and you'll be good to get settled in." Xan led the way to land.

"Um, Ms Lane? What about our gear? These are specialist cameras and lenses. What if someone tries to steal it?"

Xan laughed. "Guys, welcome to Romance Island Resort. Now you're here, there are exactly ten people on the island. The only way on or off it is via that boat – " She pointed at Baz, motoring slowly away from the jetty. " – or by helicopter, which is currently on the mainland. Unless we have a new species of shutterbug seagull, your gear will either be right here or on a trolley outside your rooms, depending on how long it takes the boys to unload the catering supplies."

The thump of twin pairs of footsteps on the jetty told her they were following, so she continued toward the main building.

She took a deep breath. "All meals are served in the staff dining room, starting with dinner tonight at seven. I'll point that out to you on the way to your accommodation. We'll meet at nine tomorrow morning to discuss your filming schedule so we can make sure you're familiar with safety at a site like this. You can ask any questions you have then, too."

"Ms Lane, we'd like to spend a few hours surveying the territory before we start filming tomorrow. Take some pictures, maybe some video, so we can decide what parts of the island will work best. Will that be a problem?"

She wasn't sure which of the men had spoken, but it didn't matter.

"Of course not," Xan replied. "Go wherever you like. With the hotel closed and no guests, it won't matter where you film, as long as you keep your cameras out of the staff bathrooms." She couldn't keep the darkness from seeping into her tone for that last part. Cameras in the women's bathroom had been an ongoing problem at the backpackers hostel she used to manage. She'd never had that problem at the resort, though maybe that was because of the extra-friendly frog population here.

SEVENTEEN

"My beach has the best view of sunset over the lagoon. When you've had your fill of me, we can take a break, and lie on the beach, watching the sunset, before we do it all over again," Jay said as he led the way between the palm trees.

Alarm bells sliced through the lusty fog in Flavia's head as she squinted up at the sun, still high in the sky. "Once only," she croaked, then cleared her throat and tried again. "That's in the papers you signed, too. The deal was to have sex once and that's all. Not all afternoon and evening, as many times as you want. That's not part of the deal."

Jay stopped so suddenly she almost ran into his back. Her nose came dangerously close to the dip between his shoulder blades before she reared back to maintain her distance.

He turned and stared at her. "You know your first time

might hurt a bit, right? And that it's better the second and maybe even the third time? You seriously think you'll only want to sleep with me once?"

No, her brain whimpered, as Flavia managed to say aloud, "That's the deal."

Honey-gold eyes held hers for what seemed like an eternity. "I don't think you know what you're getting into," he said softly. "But if you want more…when you want more, just say so. It's your deal and you set the terms. If you want something to dream about later, you won't want to just remember the pain."

Flavia swallowed as icy-cold fingers closed over her heart. Yes, of course she knew her first time would hurt. She'd been trying not to think about it, but Jay's insistence meant now she could think of nothing else. Not his hands on her or the erotic dreams that had fuelled her courage the last week. The thought of pain as he penetrated her and…would she scream? Cry? Oh God, what if she cried? She didn't want him to see her cry.

A white, sandy beach spread out before her, edged by palm trees. Flavia forced her breathing to slow. This wasn't so bad. Sex on the beach in paradise, with a rock god who had a body to match. She could do this. Just as long as he didn't see her cry.

Flavia stripped off her clothes with shaking hands and draped them over the sign confirming that this was, indeed, a private beach. Once naked, she didn't dare glance down or she'd lose her nerve. She didn't even want to meet Jay's eyes. Instead, she turned her back on him and walked toward the water. A warm wave caressed her toes, teasing her, before it retreated, tempting her to come in deeper.

Here would do. The sand was soft and Flavia could fix her eyes on the horizon as he…

She dropped to her knees in the water, then leaned forward so she was on all fours. She had to swallow three times before her voice could actually form the words. "Here. I want you to do me right here. Doggy style. Now." She forced her body to stay still, instead of shaking to pieces like she felt it wanted to.

A soft splash told her Jay was right behind her. Lightly, he touched her backside.

Flavia jerked away. "You don't get to touch my arse. That's off limits!" she barked.

"What do you want?" He ran a finger up her spine, until his hand rested on the back of her neck. "You don't want kisses. You don't want me to touch you. You seriously want me to fuck you, right here and now, without any foreplay? That's fucked up. It's not how I do things." His fingers traced circles at the nape of her neck, tickling the skin of her back as the circles grew wider. "Tell me what you want, baby."

She'd never felt so vulnerable. So small. Naked on a beach with a man behind her who she couldn't see. Flavia tensed and edged her knees wider apart on the sand. "I want you to…ffff-fuck me right here. Right now." Where had she picked up a stutter? Damn it, why was he drawing this out? Something sharp dug into her knee and Flavia focussed on the pain, which would distract her from the rising panic of anticipation of worse pain when he…

"If you don't do it right now," she continued, wincing as a wave washed over her leg and the salt turned mild discomfort into a stinging sensation across her right kneecap. She gritted her teeth. "If you don't fuck me right now, I'll go to the press. I'll tell them Jay Felix has to pay for sex. He buys virgin girls for sex. I'll say he's an impotent pussy who can't even get it up when a girl begs him for it. Quit screwing around and fuck me!" She shifted her knee, hoping to stop it from hurting but if anything, the stinging grew worse. She tried and failed to stifle a gasp.

His hands weren't touching her any more. She wanted to turn and look, but forced herself to focus her gaze on the horizon. Not the man behind her who probably needed both hands to undress himself and put on a condom.

"Are you sure?" Jay didn't sound sure. He sounded like he wanted out of this deal.

But Flavia was angry now, fuelled by rage at the pain in her knee and the agonising embarrassment that she was naked on a beach in front of this man and he still hadn't done what she asked. Wasn't she good enough for him? Not good enough for James, not good enough for anyone…she wouldn't be the Million Dollar Girl if she didn't do this. Instead, she'd be worthless. "Yes, I'm fucking sure," she snapped.

She felt his breath between her legs, on her…

"But baby, you're not ready. You're not…wait, are you bleeding? Is that blood?" His hand wrapped around her thigh, just above her knee. "It is! You're hurt. You are bleeding. It's all over the sand and in the water, too. The sand's red and it's…"

With no warning, a heavy weight descended on her back, forcing her down toward the water. She screamed, but the sound cut off with a gurgle as Jay pushed her face beneath the surface.

EIGHTEEN

The sound of screaming had Xan on her feet and running for the source before her brain had processed that it wasn't coming from a bathroom. This sounded like it was coming from Pearl Beach and, yes, while it was so high pitched it did sound like a girl, experience had taught her that screaming men didn't sound much different. She burst through the last of the palms and spotted the girl – Flavia – wrestling with Jay in the shallows, still screaming hysterically.

"Get off her, you wanker!" Xan shouted, charging in to help Flavia. Together, they shoved the surprisingly unresisting arsehole off the naked girl. Jay lay on his back in the water, unconscious. Xan was impressed. Flavia must have knocked the raping bastard out before he could even take his pants off. "Are you all right?" she asked the girl.

Shivering even in the heat, Flavia crossed the beach and

pulled her dress over her head to cover her nakedness before struggling into her underwear. Wide-eyed with fright, the girl didn't seem capable of saying a word.

Xan looked her over. She was soaking wet from head to toe, but it didn't look like she was badly injured. A streak of red trickled down her leg. Blood. Miss Chastity wasn't a virgin any more and it had taken a bastard like Jay to end that for her. She glared at Jay, but he was still out cold. Maybe she should just leave him on the beach to drown.

Running footsteps slowed as they hit the sand. "We saw everything from across the lagoon," Tim gasped out. "She shouted something at him and then he attacked her. Got here as fast as I could while Simmo…Simmo…" He flapped a hand in the direction of the far shore, where the Simon stood with a camera in hand. "Filmed everything." Tim sucked in another breath. "You can show the police what he did to her."

Xan nodded, thinking. "Help me get him out of the water. Bring him up the beach a bit so he doesn't drown." He deserved to, but Xan decided to leave him to the mercies of the criminal justice system instead. She'd send him to the police to sort out.

She grabbed one arm, Tim grabbed the other, and together they dragged Jay's body up to the path. Next, she pulled out her phone, then changed her mind and tapped her wristband instead. She scrolled through the options until she found the option she'd insisted IT create for the owner – his initials, JF. The alert zipped straight to Maintenance, alerting Lee to get a trolley big enough to carry Jay when he'd drunk himself into a stupor so deep he wouldn't wake up, plus enough cleaning supplies to deal with the mess he usually left behind. A quick check told her Jay was still breathing, as he always was, and for once he didn't reek of alcohol and vomit. He'd probably been washed clean in the water, that's why, Xan mused.

She rose and addressed Tim: "You and Simon, head back to the main building. Get hold of the IT guys. I want you to download whatever footage you have of this incident so we can give it to the police. Tell Seb and Cam – the IT guys – to recall the helicopter. Say it's urgent." She looked at pale-faced Flavia. "Take her with you. See if you can get her to drink a cup of tea in the staff dining room. Make sure she's okay."

Tim eyed her and the wretched rock star. "Are you sure you'll be okay with him? What if he gets violent again?"

Xan scanned the beach until she found what she wanted. Crossing to the pile of driftwood, she hefted a piece that would make a suitable club. She smacked one end into her palm. "Then I'll clout him again." She hoped Jay gave her the opportunity this time, but when he was out, he was out for hours. "I'll be fine. I've alerted Maintenance and they'll be here shortly to help me."

Tim nodded. After a polite, "Ladies first," to Flavia, he followed the girl back through the foliage to the hotel.

Xan crouched beside Jay, leaning over to delicately sniff his breath. He really didn't smell like he'd been drinking at all. Why, then, had he tried to force a girl into having sex with him? Had she panicked partway through when he hurt her – the tell-tale blood on her leg – and decided she didn't want to go through with it after all? That's what must have happened. Jay, being the entitled arsehole he was, would have made a brutish comment about how he'd paid for her, so he'd have her, and she'd had to fight him off. What had she hit him with, though? It's not like there were any rocks or driftwood clubs within reach of where they'd been struggling in the water.

If he didn't come to before the helicopter arrived, Shou would have to take him to hospital instead of the police station. The Emergency Department could check him over under the watchful eyes of Broome Police. She'd call them the moment Shou and Jay were in the air and on their way so whoever was on duty could meet them the moment Shou landed.

Bloody hell. Just what she didn't need right now. Jay had this horrible way of messing everything up – even her Easter weekend. At least this hadn't happened in front of guests. Once he was safely locked up, no one at the hotel would be in danger from the arsehole.

If he was stupid enough to try forcing himself on one girl, how many of his conquests had been bullied the same way? What if some of the hotel staff who'd left had also been raped by him? She didn't need this kind of bad press for the resort. Not now she was about to embark on a major PR campaign. She should just kill him, push him back into the water and let the waves do the work for her. It would be justice. It would…

"Ms Lane?" Lee said softly. "I brought a wheelbarrow when I saw the location of your report. Can you help me lift Mr Felix in?"

He tipped the wheelbarrow on an angle so the lip lay flush with the sand. Together, the two of them heaved, panted, struggled and swore until they'd managed to get Jay's limp body mostly into the wheelbarrow. His arms and legs hung over the sides, as usual, but the bulk of his weight was in there. It took all of their combined strength to push the barrow through the powdery sand to the paved path, where Lee could manage the load on his own. "To Villa Penguin, Ms Lane?"

Xan shook her head. "No. To the helipad this time. Better get him to hospital. I think he hit his head." There was no sign of blood or bruising, but maybe it was too early for a swelling to form. That was something the doctors could deal with. Not her problem. If he died of internal bleeding, it would be his own damn fault.

NINETEEN

Jason woke with his head pounding. No, this time the pounding was outside his head – it wasn't hurting like a hangover. What the fuck had happened? What was that thumping sound?

He pried one eye open and examined his surroundings. Hmm. A glass ceiling. That wasn't normal. Curved, too, and it felt like the ground was moving, lifting.

A voice he could only hear faintly over the thumping: "Broome Tower, this is Victor Hotel – "

Fuck. How'd he get in a helicopter? He was supposed to be having sex with some chick on the beach. The angry one who'd wanted it doggy-style, rough as guts, when he'd planned on taking it slowly. There'd been blood in the water from a cut on her leg and then he'd…FUCK.

"Where the fuck are you taking me? I'm not leaving this fucking island!" Jason sat up and glared at Shou.

Shou's tone didn't change from its flat calm. "Relax, Mr Felix. You've taken a blow to the head. Ms Lane called me to take you to hospital. Just lie back and I'll soon have you in the capable hands of – "

"Not that fucking matron! She wants to get her hands on my dick!" When Jason realised that described most of the Australian female population – Miss Chastity included – he added, "She wants to stick things in it. She's fucked-up kinky in a bad way. I'm not going back to her."

"Mr Felix, refasten your seatbelt, please. You need to keep it on until we're safely on the ground at Broome Airport."

Jason leaned over the seat so he could really get in the pilot's face. "I said I'm not going to any fucking hospital. Or town. Put this fucking helicopter back on my island now!"

"I can't, Mr Felix. Ms Lane said I couldn't come back until I'd handed you to..." The last few words were mumbled too low for Jason to hear them.

"Who did Xan say to hand me to? Is she good buddies with Madam Matron?" Jason demanded.

Shou swallowed. "The police, Mr Felix. She said you'd hurt a girl and they'll arrest you when we land. I just had to get you to the mainland."

"What fucking girl?"

Shou's hands shook on the stick, thought the helicopter still rose steadily. "The one I brought here earlier this afternoon. The one who thought I was going to drive her out to the middle of nowhere and dump her body in the desert, when you – "

"I didn't do anything to her! I never touched her! I fucking passed out and woke up here with you!" Jason didn't know what to do. He'd never had to deal with anything like this on his own before. That's what the band had a manager for. A manager and PR and scary Trevor the ex-Marine security guy. He needed to call someone and get them to figure this mess out. "Get me on the ground."

"Flight time to Broome is – "

"Now! Put me back on the ground now or I'm jumping out of your fucking helicopter!" Jason peered out the window at the water below. It looked deep enough to drop into, and he'd been in the swim squad back at school. Swimming back to the island would be like a couple lengths of the lagoon.

"Mr Felix, please."

"Fucking bird. Down. Now."

"Ms Lane will kill me."

I'll kill you, Jason thought, but he knew he wouldn't. Violence wasn't his style. "I'll handle the hotel manager. Now put this bird back on my helipad." When the pilot hesitated, Jason reached over him and grabbed the stick, tilting the helicopter down.

"No! We'll crash! Sit down, Mr Felix, so I can land us safely!"

Green flashed through one window as the helicopter tilted at an alarming angle before the pilot straightened them out.

Jason saw someone sprinting along the path, headed for the helipad. Probably Xan, ready to tackle him to the ground. No, she'd probably set some of the grounds or security staff on him – wouldn't want to dirty her hands with him. Fine. As soon as they were low enough, he'd jump onto the roof or something and surprise them.

They were level with the treetops now – it was now or never. Jason cracked open the door. Shou howled a protest, but Jay couldn't hear him over the noise of the blades and the wind rushing past. Just like he'd seen people do in movies, Jay wrapped his hands around the metal strut below the door and swung his body out the door, so he hung from the helicopter by his hands. Fuck, what a rush. Like skydiving only without the falling. Right. There was the roof where he played golf on top of Xan's office. A perfect landing spot. He swung his legs, wanting to get the angle just right.

On the count of three, he told himself. One, two…

The helicopter tilted again and his hand slipped, so he was only hanging on with one hand. Fuck. Couldn't hold the weight. Had to let go. Curl up into a ball, roll with the impact, hope he didn't break anything…

Jason landed in the crown of a palm tree, but the tree wasn't strong enough to take his weight, so as he grasped at anything his hands touched, the fronds were inexorably tipping him toward the ground. He wrapped his arms and legs around the trunk and held on for dear life.

A clang and a crack echoed across the island and something black whipped away into the jungle, only a few metres away from him. Jason heard the warning beeps from the open door of the helicopter, as it skewed sideways through the palm trees toward the helipad.

He slid to the ground, remembering to bend his knees to absorb the impact, before crouching low behind a tree as he waited for the helicopter to explode.

Seconds passed. Then a minute. Two. Maybe not all crashed helicopters exploded after all.

"You broke my baby and made her crash!" The shriek came from the direction the helicopter had gone in. Where a furious Shou was running from. "I'll kill you!"

Jason had had enough. He'd just been accused of a crime he didn't commit – one Xan wanted him arrested for – and he'd just survived jumping out of a helicopter before it crashed and the pilot was angry? Fuck that.

"You just tried to kidnap a fucking rock star from his home!" Jason roared, unleashing the full power of his voice over the island like it was an arena full of screaming fans. "If I want to burn your fucking helicopter and send you to prison for the rest of your fucked-up life, I will! Now shut the fuck up. Where's Xan?" He sucked in a deep breath and bellowed, "Xan Lane! Get your arse out here! I want some fucking answers!"

TWENTY

The sounds of the helicopter faded as Xan turned her attention to the four men huddled around the biggest monitor in the room. "Yep, you can see it clearly," Simon said, pointing. "Right here." A girl's voice, shouting indistinctly, then screaming a few seconds later. A pause, then more screaming. "He made her take her clothes off, get down in the water, and when she shouted at him to stop, he shoved her down and forced himself on her. Shit. That's…messed up."

Not as messed up as seeing them struggling firsthand, Xan thought. "Show me," she demanded, and the men parted to allow her to see the screen. It was pretty much as they'd described it. They'd been filming a slow panorama across the lagoon, but when they heard shouting, the camera zeroed in on the couple, just in time for some grainy footage of Jay landing on top of Flavia.

"Can you do anything with the sound so we can hear what she shouted?" Xan asked.

The men all looked at each other, then Tim frowned. "I can think of a couple of software programs that might be able to help. Do you have an internet connection here?"

Cam and Seb almost fell over themselves to assure him there was and opened a web browser on the big screen for him.

Xan waited impatiently for a few minutes while nothing happened before she said, "How long will this take?"

Tim shrugged. "Once it downloads, anything from a few minutes to a few hours, depending on how much cleanup is required for the audio. No way to tell until we start."

Xan help up her phone. "Right. You keep working on it, then. Call me when you have something." Speaking of making calls, she needed to phone Broome Police Station to make sure they were ready to greet Jay when he landed. But she could do that in the comfort of her office, or even her flat, instead of here.

Office, she decided, striding down the corridor to the foyer. She'd left her computer on and she may as well shut everything down properly, seeing as she had no intention of doing any further work after she knocked off. In about another fifteen minutes. She dialled the number as she closed her email.

"Broom Police Station, Constable Nelson speaking."

"Hi, Naomi. It's Xan, over at Romance Island Resort."

Xan could almost hear Naomi smiling into the phone. "Have you killed him yet? That up-himself celebrity who lost his licence on the Labour Day weekend? Or has he flown home and out of your hair?"

Jay had lost his licence, huh? That might explain why he'd stayed at the resort so much instead of picking up fangirls at the pubs in town.

"Funny you should mention him. There's been…an incident here at the hotel. I'm trying to find out more, but he invited a guest to stay with him, which is fine, but today one of our staff found them wrestling and the girl knocked him unconscious."

Naomi whistled. "Did you buy the girl a beer? Ask her what it felt like?"

Xan winced. "Not really. She's not saying much. I think she's still in shock. Look, like I said, we're still trying to work out what happened, but at the moment, we suspect rape. One of the cameras at the resort caught some of the incident and we've got our IT guys trying to clean up the footage to see what actually happened. He's still unconscious, so I got a couple of the guys to carry him into the helicopter. Shou's on his way to the airport with him now. He definitely assaulted the girl – nearly drowned her, in fact. I had to pull him off her. Will that be enough for you to charge him when he arrives?"

"I told him I'd arrest him on sight if he showed his face in town again, so sure. When did you say he left the island?"

Xan checked her watch. "Maybe ten, fifteen minutes ago? Plenty of time for you to beat him to the airport."

"I'll need to take witness statements. How long is the victim staying at the resort?"

Xan choked out a laugh. "I think she'll want to be on the next ride out, to be honest, but I can – "

An almighty crash outside stopped her in her tracks. Now what?

"One sec, Naomi. Something's happened outside and I need to check it out. Can I call you back?"

Silence was her only reply.

"Naomi?"

More silence.

Xan hung up the phone. She had another disaster to sort out. At least this one couldn't possibly involve Jay fucking Felix.

TWENTY-ONE

"Xan!"

She bolted out of the main building, then skidded to a halt at the sight of him. "What in Hell are you doing here? You should be halfway to Broome by now!"

"This is my fucking island," Jason spat. "I live here. What kind of bullshit story did you spin to the pilot to get him to take me to Broome? Said I'd hurt some girl? I never hurt a single fucking girl in my life!" He glared at her. "Good thing, too. 'Cause if you were a man, I'd deck you right here and now." He was so furious, he fucking meant it, too.

Xan looked like she wanted to take a step back, but she didn't. "Oh yeah? What about Miss Chastity, your little girl friend? The one you almost drowned this afternoon?"

"What the fuck are you on about? I barely touched her!"

Xan straightened with a righteous sniff. "Don't bullshit

me. I saw you. It took two of us to get you off her and that's after she knocked you out."

"She didn't knock me out!" Jason protested. "I fucking fainted, that's all!"

Xan snorted. "Yeah, right. You expect me to believe the big, bad rock star banged that poor girl, then had a fit of the vapours and fainted?"

Jason opened his mouth to defend himself, but Xan wasn't through yet.

"I saw the blood trickling down her leg. Your little virgin isn't one any more. From what I saw, it didn't look good. Rape's still illegal, even if you're paying the girl for sex. Or did she hit you so hard that you forgot about that?"

Jason had no words. His mouth gaped open, as vacant as his mind right now. Was this some kind of fucked-up dream? It had to be. Nothing made sense in it. He just wanted to wake up so it would end.

Now he understood Angel's nightmares.

Jason swallowed and lowered his voice. "We were just getting started on foreplay when I fainted, all right? I think she cut herself on a shell or something. We didn't do anything. Not yet. Fuck." He ran his fingers through his hair, and came up with leaves. He threw them on the ground. "Did she tell you this shit? Just what I need. Another fucked-up, crazy bitch. She said you'd checked her police clearance, but I guess you missed the crazy part. Where is she now?"

Xan pressed her lips together. "Like I'd tell you, after what I saw."

Jason was tired of arguing. "Just fucking ask her. Say you've already talked to me and my lawyers will make fucking mincemeat of her if she tries lying."

"I will." Xan's expression turned from angry to suspicious. "How come you're not in the helicopter, anyway? Did you threaten Shou if he didn't let you out before he took off?"

Jason managed a smug smile. "Nope. I jumped out."

The shock on Xan's face was worth every ache he'd have tomorrow. "You did what? Jumped out of a flying helicopter? How did you manage that without killing yourself?" she demanded.

"I knew what I was doing. I aimed for the roof, right over your office. I know every centimetre of it from playing golf up there."

Xan's breath hissed out like an angry snake. "So the crash I heard earlier was you, throwing yourself out of a helicopter? Bloody hell, Jay, you're lucky you didn't break something."

He decided not to mention the helicopter.

Xan closed her eyes, then looked to the skies as if hoping for answers. "All right. I'll go ask her what happened. She hasn't said a word yet, for the record. I only know what I saw, and what I saw was you on top of her and her struggling to get free. Just..." She clenched her hands, like she wished they were around his throat. "Go into my office and wait for me there while I decide whether to call the police to bring their helicopter over here to arrest you. Your rock star reputation won't protect you if you're as full of shit as I think you are." When Jason didn't move, she stamped her foot. "GO! I'm not moving until you're inside."

Jason shrugged and ambled into the foyer. When he

glanced back outside, she'd gone.

Good. He had a crazy girl to locate. If the rape story Xan spouted was second-hand, he needed to hear it from the source. He strode down the corridor to IT.

The IT population had doubled – Seb and Cam had two other guys in there, all watching some video. Jason glanced at it and was stunned to see a grainy recording of his own fainting fit. He fell flat on top of the poor girl in the water.

Fuck. That explained the drowning bit. But rape? Really? The video would show he'd barely touched her.

"Rewind that and play it again from the beginning," Jason demanded.

All four men jumped. Seb and Cam's gazes slid away to look anywhere but at him, while the other two seemed frozen in place.

"Jay…Felix?" one of them managed to say.

Jason grunted his assent.

"The manager said there weren't any guests at the island, so we could video wherever we wanted. We had no idea…" the guy gushed.

Jason jerked his head at the video. "Could've fooled me. Looks like you were filming me and my friend with your zoom lens while we were on our private beach. Show me what you got."

Shock turned the guy's face paler than beach sand. "Y-yes, Mr Felix. Right away."

Several seconds later, Jason watched in horrified fascination as the camera panned around the lagoon, taking in rocks, waves and secluded beaches, before unintelligible shouting drew the cameraman's attention to the source. There she was, on her hands and knees in the surf, and

Jason saw himself straighten and take a step away from her, before keeling over on top of her, like a skittle in a bowling alley. Fuck. He watched the girl struggling to get out from under him before Xan appeared to join in the battle.

What happened to first aid? To fucking checking the unconscious patient first? Jason turned away from the screen. He understood what Xan thought she'd seen, but she was dead wrong. And if she didn't believe him, he'd make the girl tell the truth. Fuck, he didn't even know her name.

"Where is she?" Jason demanded.

"The hotel manager told me to take her to the staff dining room to have tea, so I did," the cameraman volunteered.

Tea. Trust English Xan to suggest something as silly as tea. Crazy girls didn't sit at a table drinking tea.

Jason pointed at Cam. "Use her ID. Find her."

Cam nodded shakily and his fingers skittered across the keys of the nearest computer. "Helipad," he said breathlessly.

Where the helicopter crashed. Oh fuck. He set off at a run. The last thing Jason wanted was for the girl to die in the crash he'd caused.

TWENTY-TWO

Flavia blinked at the uncomfortably hot Styrofoam cup in her hands. She was slowly recovering from the shock of…what exactly had happened? Jay had shoved her under the water, but when she and the hotel manager had managed to free her, he was out cold. Had the manager hit him? Flavia didn't think so. Tangled with him the way she was, she'd have felt the impact of a blow. Unless she hit him before he'd landed on her, and that's why he fell…

She shook her head. It didn't matter. This whole mess had turned into a disaster of epic proportions. Yet here she was, nursing a cup of tea that she had no intention of drinking.

Flavia knew what to do when disaster struck. It was time to cut her losses and head back to Perth, so she could catch a plane to Bali. Days of cocktails by the pool with the girls would soon banish this bad dream from her mind. Bugger virginity auctions and men in general. Her first time would be on her terms and the bloke would consider himself bloody lucky to have her.

Flavia rose. She dusted off her dress, though the salt-stiffened fabric resisted her efforts at smoothing it. She should probably change clothes before she left the island. She needed to retrieve her bag, too. Hoping Jay wouldn't be home, she slipped out of the staff canteen and followed the path around the lagoon. She found his villa after a couple of wrong turns, but the door stymied her until she remembered her wristband – the one she still wore, despite the struggle on the beach. Not expecting the waterlogged wristband to work, she waved it at the scanner and gasped when the door slid open.

Her bag was right where she'd left it: beside her chair. The document-littered dining table brought her up short. She needed the signed contracts, just in case. Sweeping the mess of papers back into her folder, she shoved the whole thing into her bag and zipped it up. There. She thought about changing clothes, but decided against it. She'd be soaked in sweat after five minutes outside, anyway, and hours of plane travel would only crumple it worse than it was now. She'd change when she reached the hotel in Bali. When her holiday would truly start.

Until then…she had a plane to catch. But first, the helicopter.

Holding her head high, Flavia marched out of the villa, her suitcase dogging her heels.

She found the helipad gate on her first try, thanks to the signs pointing the way. The helicopter was home, too, but empty. She sat on her suitcase to wait.

The weather had other ideas. The clouds overhead decided to dump their load on her head, unable to wait any longer. Swearing, Flavia made a dash for the nearest shelter: the inside of the helicopter. The door clicked open, allowing her entry, before she slammed it shut behind her. There. The rain couldn't get her now.

But boredom could. Flavia hauled her bag onto the seat beside her and pulled out the paperwork. On top was the no-kissing, no-kinky-stuff contract she and Violet had dreamed up together to put him off, but it hadn't worked. Worthless now. Seizing the pages in both hands, she ripped the contract in two. There. She flung the paper on the floor. The deal was off. She was free to join her friends and have fun for once.

Flavia pulled out her phone. She should probably call Violet to tell her the good news. Depressing the power button, she waited for the screen to chime into life. The error message across it wasn't what she wanted, though — it said there was no network connection and only emergency calls could be made. She held it up, moving it around the cramped cabin, trying to get a signal, but no matter how many times she made her phone search for a network, it found none. When she got to Broome, then. When she could book the next available flight out of here and onward to Bali.

Movement caught her eye and she peered out into the rain to see what it was. A blurry figure approached the helicopter. He cracked open the door.

"Finally!" Flavia exclaimed. "I thought you'd leave me waiting here forever. I have a flight to catch. How soon until we leave?"

"That eager to get out of here?"

It wasn't the pilot.

"You spun a story about rape to the staff here so I'd be arrested, and by the time the police think to question the witness, you're long gone with my money." Jay reached into her folder of papers and pulled out the envelope. He seemed sad. "It was all about the money, wasn't it? I mean, the contract means nothing to you." He eyed the ripped pages.

Flavia stared at the envelope. "I didn't mean to take that. It must have been between the rest of the papers on the table when I gathered them up. I…can't take that. I didn't…didn't…deliver the goods, as promised. I didn't mean for any of this to happen. I wasn't even going to go through with the auction. I was going to call it off and then it ended and you…" She swallowed. "I'm sorry. This didn't turn out anything like I expected."

"Yeah, me neither. Are you even a virgin?"

"Yes!"

Jay snorted. "So you're going back on the auction block now? When we had a deal?"

"NO!" It came out louder than Flavia expected. "I never intended to do it. I tried to cancel the auction before it ended. It was a mistake." She laughed weakly. "And while I was sitting at my desk, panicking that I'd ended the thing instead of cancelling it, the auction winner sent me an email with a picture of him as a magazine centrefold attached." Her cheeks grew unnaturally hot. "I thought it was a joke at first, but the more research I did, the more I realised that it was actually you. I couldn't say no to you."

Jay's scowl broke into a grin. "You internet stalked me

after I emailed you? Really?" He swung into the co-pilot's seat and shut the door. "So at what point did you decide to frame me for rape? Or was it blackmail you planned?" He leaned over the back of the seat, closer and more than a little scary.

Flavia shrank back, shaking her head violently. "Nothing like that. I haven't said anything to anyone. You pushed me under the water and the next thing I knew, the hotel manager was pulling me out and you were unconscious."

"Unconscious. Yeah. About that." Jay retreated and scratched his chin. "I must've tripped and fell. Must have hit my head somehow. Yeah." He nodded vigorously. "Sorry I fell on you. That…sort of fucked things up, didn't it? Wasn't part of the plan. I pictured this going very differently."

"That makes two of us." The longer he looked into her eyes, the less she could think about anything else. Or anyone else. "Don't you wish we could just start today over again?"

Jay laughed. "Fuck no. I jumped out of a helicopter today. My first time. It was awesome."

Flavia couldn't help laughing. What kind of crazy man jumped out of helicopters for fun? A gorgeous, rich rock star who lived in paradise. Not the sort of man she normally had anything to do with. Her laughter died. "I just wanted things to be different. More like a dream than a nightmare."

"So how was it in your dreams, then?" Jay winked. "Just us here, no one else. I'll keep your secrets, I promise. What happens at Romance Island stays at Romance Island, or at least I think that's what it says on the brochure someone left on my desk to approve. Tell me your dreams, baby." Honey eyes captured her in their spell.

Flavia hesitated. This was a man who jumped out of helicopters for fun, she told herself. Who had more sex after one concert than she'd had in her entire life. He probably had the *Kama Sutra* memorised. "More romance, I guess."

"Oh, you wanted hearts and chocolates, flowers and dinner?" Jay shrugged. "I can do some of that, at least. Come back to my place and I'll get the chef to sort out dinner and chocolate. I could probably pick some flowers, as long as you don't mind a few frogs, and the resort has this incredible orgy pack that comes in a heart-shaped box. Condoms in every flavour, with lickable lubes to match, and some toys even I haven't worked out where to put."

Blushing furiously, Flavia didn't know what to say. Finally, she found her voice. "Not…kinky stuff and food. I mean…" Oh God, he was going to make her say it.

"Dancing? Serenading you on your balcony? Love letters? Bad poetry? Watching soppy chick flicks until I hurl?"

He had her laughing again. "No. I meant…foreplay."

Understanding dawned in those eyes, turning them into twin golden suns. "You mean all the stuff you said you didn't want me to do in the contract you made me sign?" His eyes strayed to the ripped pages. "The one that doesn't apply any more?" Wicked suns transfixed her in their beam.

"No, it doesn't," she admitted reluctantly.

"So I can kiss you now?"

"I suppose —"

She didn't get to finish and she didn't want to, either.

Hot lips melted hers apart, leaving her gasping for breath. His tongue beckoned hers and the dance began, as Jay led masterfully and she followed. Her lips bloomed as her heart kept time to a lively beat that made the rest of her body long to join in. Jay tasted of salt and promises and…

Flavia broke away. "I can't," she panted.

Jay grinned. "In my professional opinion, I think you can. I think you can do anything you want to. What do you want, baby?"

Oh God, he knew she wanted him. She could read it in his eyes. It couldn't hurt to tell him what he already knew. It wouldn't change anything. "I wish I could have you, just once, before I have to leave."

Jay spread his arms. "We're here now. You can have me right here, if you want."

"Here? In a helicopter?"

"I've always wondered what it'd be like to have sex in a helicopter. This'll be my first time."

Flavia managed a faint smile. "Mine, too."

Jay reached out and caressed her face. "Two things first, baby. We try things my way. Anything you don't like, you say so, but when you do like what I do to you…let me know, all right?"

She nodded.

Jay climbed over the seat and took her in his arms. His mouth, his hands, his whole damn body were everywhere, burning her dreams into faint memories as he set her insides on fire in the most delicious ways. She stretched out across the seats, helpless in his hands as she savoured every moment.

"So what do you think, baby?"

Flavia's blissful fog cleared enough for her to focus on his laughing eyes. "I think all the stories were true." She sucked in a deep breath. "You're the most legendary lover who ever lived."

Jay burst out laughing. "Baby, that was just the beginning. A taste…or what you called it, foreplay. Would you like some more?"

Before she could think, her head nodded. "I want more…of you. I want to feel you inside me."

"Baby, I've been inside you. You taste delicious." One finger slid between her legs and out again before he popped it into his mouth.

"I want…I don't want to be a virgin any more. And I want my first time to be with you." She attempted a smile through her nervousness. "Our first time…together in a helicopter."

"How can I say no to an offer like that?" His shorts joined her clothes on the floor before he sheathed his rigid length in red latex. "Strawberry flavoured. Are you sure you're ready for this, baby?"

Flavia flung her legs over the seat backs, so they spread wide in invitation. "Yes." She meant it, too. "Make me into a woman, Jay." Just being able to say his name while staring at the body she'd only seen in pictures sent a thrill deep inside her.

He shifted so he knelt between her legs, the tip of his cock teasing her. "Easy does it, baby." He parted her like some biblical sea in one long, slow thrust. "Are you all right?"

Flavia shifted her hips, tilting them up to meet him. "Yes. I thought I'd hurt more, but…oh God, that feels so good."

Jay moved inside her, each thrust as tortuously slow as the first until she couldn't take it any more.

"Faster, please," she begged.

But he didn't relent. Slowly, steadily, her orgasm built around him as his hands and his mouth drove the rest of her to distraction. Too much. It was too much and too incredible and oh God this time she was going to explode. The rest of the world could go to hell because it was just her and Jay, making her whole body sing for joy.

She screamed his name to the heavens.

TWENTY-THREE

"Oh my GOD…James, James!"

At first, he thought it was his name she was screaming, until he realised it was some other bloke's. Fuck. He finished quickly, wanting to get the fuck away from her. He threw the condom on the pilot's seat, reached for his shorts and noticed the envelope on the seat beside them.

"Now you got what you came for, you'll be leaving, right?" he asked bitterly.

Her eyes were still closed, probably so she could imagine he was some other fucker. A fucker called James.

"Mmm-hmm."

Jason's heart froze within his chest. So much for being this girl's fantasy. He cracked open the door, letting the evening breeze clear his head. "Here." He tossed the envelope on her bare belly, slick with sweat from their frenzied…fucking. Because it wasn't anything else. Just physical. No emotional connection at all because she spent the whole time wishing he was someone else. "You earned it, Miss Chastity."

He couldn't stand being near her any more. Clambering out of the helicopter, he let the rain wash him clean. The stinging drops were nothing compared to the needling pain inside. What was the point in being some girl's first and best if she'd never remember it was him? Slinging his shorts over his shoulder, he set off through the jungle to his lonely villa.

TWENTY-FOUR

Xan kept checking to make sure Jay wasn't following her before she backtracked and took the path that led to the staff dining room. She wanted to talk to Flavia alone, so she could hear the girl's story without any interference from Jay. She might not like the man, but she had to admit she'd never thought of him as a sexual predator. A sex maniac and a shameless opportunist, yes, but not someone to fear. Now, though…

But the staff dining room was empty except for a forlorn white cup of untouched tea. Where had the girl gone?

Xan stuck her head in the kitchen and asked the chef, but he just shrugged and said he hadn't seen her. He was too busy preparing dinner for the remaining staff to take any notice of what was going on outside his kitchen. With a pointed look at the simmering pots on the stove, he turned his back on Xan.

Bloody hell, this was a mess. Xan returned to her office, breaking into a run when the rain started. So much for finishing work early for the weekend. It was times like this she wondered if Jay Felix was the devil himself, sent to torment her into killing him. He didn't do a damn thing she said. He wasn't in the office waiting for her, like he was supposed to be. Did that mean he was busily searching the island for Flavia so he could finish what he started?

She reached for her phone and cradled the receiver between her cheek and her shoulder as she dialled. Who first? IT to locate Flavia's wristband, or the Broome police to tell them their suspect had escaped and was now at large on the island?

Flavia first, she decided. Once the girl was safe, then she could worry about getting assistance to apprehend the arsehole.

She dialled the IT extension and waited. And waited. The phone didn't ring or beep or make any sound at all. Flavia hung up and tried again. Nothing, not even a dial tone. She slammed the receiver down. Fine. She'd email them instead. Her computer booted up quickly, as if sensing her urgency. Her email program wasn't as helpful, though — it spent forever checking for new messages. Finally, it flashed up exactly one new message — an error, telling her she didn't have a network connection.

Phones down. Internet down. Mobiles had been down since the last storm and the repair guy wasn't due for another week. It was like fate was deliberately isolating them on the island with a crazy man. All…ten of them, including Jay. She shivered. Wasn't there an Agatha Christie book about ten people trapped on an island with a psychopath? Didn't they all die?

If she made it through this weekend, she swore to hunt the book down. And knock Jay out with it.

In the meantime, she'd have to visit the IT guys in person and hope the wristband GPS system still worked. Crossing the dimly lit foyer, she almost shrieked when a shadow staggered into her path. It took her a few seconds to recognise the soaked, shaking figure as Shou.

"What happened to you?" she asked.

"He made me break my baby. I crashed her!" Shou hid his face in his hands and let out what sounded like a sob.

He had children? He'd never mentioned kids before. Where was their mother? Flavia gave herself a mental shake as she realised what he meant. Everyone knew the pilot was practically married to his helicopter. Which meant… "You crashed the helicopter? Where? Are you all right?" She yanked him under one of the downlights so she could check him for injuries.

Shou jerked out of her grip. "I'm fine. But your…boss…attacked me during take-off, then opened the door and fell out. I managed to get my baby under control and steered her away from the buildings, but we were too low. I clipped a tree. I tried to correct, but the rotors hit something metal and it sheared off one of the blades. Then I wasn't flying any more, more like falling, and wrestling her down before we crashed. He made me crash my baby and he said he'd burn her!"

Make that two crazy men. And now, there was no way off the island. "Where did you crash? Do I need to send out a firefighting crew?" Xan stared out into the worsening storm, wondering if it would be more effective than any crew she could muster. She had horrible visions of the two IT guys with one limp hose between them as an inferno burned out of control through the jungle.

Shou straightened. "Of course not. I'm the best helicopter pilot in the Southern Hemisphere. My broken baby's on the helipad, waiting for repairs so she can fly again."

Xan's heart sank. "So with that on the helipad, there's no way we can get another helicopter in or out. We're basically stuck here with the crazy man who attacked you and a girl, and we have no idea who'll be next."

"Maybe we could barricade ourselves in the cyclone shelter? Call for reinforcements, lock all the doors and bunker down until help arrives?" Shou suggested.

He was a pilot, Xan reminded herself. A good one who'd just been through a traumatic experience. It wasn't his fault communications were down. Or was it? "Where did you say you were when you lost a rotor? The jungle between the main building and the helipad, right?" Where the satellite dish compound stood, hedged by a metal fence.

"Yes."

The helicopter or one of the broken-off bits must have hit the satellite dish, while the fence built to defend the dish wreaked havoc on the helicopter. All because of the bloody rock star who couldn't keep his bits in his pants. So much for crazy men being the biggest danger. Jay was enough to turn her homicidal.

But Shou made eleven, so this wasn't a murder mystery any more.

Xan's breath hissed out. "Okay, it looks like you're stuck

in this mess along with the rest of us. I need to find the girl, and Jay, but after that, I'll find somewhere for you to stay until we can raise someone on the mainland. There's a radio at the pearl farm, right?"

Shou nodded.

Xan strode to IT, not bothering to knock. Her footsteps on the tiles announced her arrival long before she swept through the door. "I need you to find the girl. She should still have her wristband – "

"Already on it, Ms Lane. Last scan before the internet went down, she was at the helipad, but that was over an hour ago."

An hour? Really? Time flew when you were dealing with disasters. Who knew?

"What systems have we lost, aside from the internet?" She had to know. Once she knew all the bad news, maybe she'd get some that was good.

Cam didn't meet her eyes. "Internet. Phones. GPS tracking. In-house movies and all the TV channels."

No adult movies for the IT guys and Jay. What a tragedy. "Does anything work?"

"We still have power, and the local network's up. That's mostly door locks and scanners at the bar and restaurant," Seb chimed in, a grin plastered on his face.

Not enough to find Flavia. "I'll head out to the helipad, then. I may as well assess the damage while I'm there."

Simon cleared his throat. "Actually, Tim's already out there. He said he wanted to keep an eye on Mr Felix."

"Jay was HERE?" Xan closed her mouth before she shouted anything else. A deep breath. Two. A third. Now, calmly, she continued, "Mr Felix was here. Do you know where he went?"

"The helipad, where the girl was. That's where he said he was going." Simon smiled. "I'm sure Tim has everything under control."

Xan had a horrible image of the cameraman and the rock star, facing off on the helipad in the pouring rain. Her tally of crazy men rose from two to three. She glanced around the room. No, to six. Was there a single sane man on the island?

No. Shit like this made her doubt her own sanity. Maybe she should have stayed at the backpackers with the frogs and the fly-in/fly-out boys, after all.

Instead, she headed out into the rain, heartily cursing Romance Island Resort and its rock star owner.

TWENTY-FIVE

Flavia's body buzzed, still riding the high brought on by Jay Felix. The stories fell far short of the euphoric reality. A million champagne bubbles burst in her blood.

His words permeated her blissful fog: "You earned it." Something cool touched her belly, then fluttered up to her breasts when a warm breeze gusted in. Flavia pushed it aside, not wanting anything to distract her from savouring the feel of Jay's caresses.

Warm droplets pattered onto her foot, waking her up. Had Jay decided to wash her clean afterwards?

But Jay was nowhere in sight. The helicopter door gaped into the darkening evening light, letting in rain and wind and the biggest mosquitoes she'd ever seen. Flavia grabbed her clothes and dressed in record time.

Now she noticed the thing she'd pushed aside was an envelope. The one with her money in it, making her the

Million Dollar Girl in truth.

You earned it.

And, just like that, her euphoria vanished, leaving a yawning canyon of horror. She might have more than a million dollars to her name, but never had she felt so cheap. Tears sprang to her eyes, rubbing salt into the wounds of her terrible mistake.

No, not just hers. Jay did this to her. Turned her into a cheap hooker with his hands and his money and his honey eyes. She wanted to get as far away from him as possible. The other side of the world, maybe.

So where was the damn pilot, the one who could fly her away from here?

Flavia slid out of the helicopter, her feet splashing ankle-deep into the flood engulfing the helipad. She sloshed to the gate before she realised she wasn't alone. A shadowy figure stood on the path. The pilot, surely. It had to be. No one else would be crazy enough to be out in this downpour. "Are we taking off soon?" she shouted to be heard over the rain.

"That thing's not going anywhere soon. One of the blades is missing." He pointed.

Flavia squinted back at the helicopter. Her heart stuttered to a stop when she realised he was right. "Then how do I get off this accursed island? I have a flight to catch. I need to go!"

He shrugged. "I think you're stuck here for the night, right along with the rest of us. Walk up to Reception with me and we'll see if the hotel manager can find you a room for the night."

A room? That meant she'd need her bag. Flavia begged

him to wait, then climbed back into the helicopter to fetch her things. Once she had her bag in hand, she hurried after him, dragging the suitcase through the puddles behind her.

They reached the veranda around the main building and he stepped from darkness to yellow glowing light. It wasn't the pilot at all.

"Tim!" Flavia exclaimed. "What were you doing, standing out there by the helipad in the rain?"

He shook the water from his hair, his mouth twisting into an unhappy smile. "I followed Mr Felix out there, seeing as we figured he might get violent again. I thought I might have to be your knight in shining armour. I wasn't expecting a show."

Flavia flushed, mortified. "You mean you watched us have sex?"

Tim shrugged. "Wasn't much to see, love. What with you two steaming up the windows and all. There was the tell-tale way you had the helicopter rocking, of course. And I heard you loud and clear. You sure can scream." He shook his head. "This afternoon, you might have had me fooled, but tonight I knew what I was hearing. That was no scream for help. It was a scream for more."

Flavia wanted the earth to swallow her up. "You saw us this afternoon on the beach, too?"

"Baby, everyone on the island saw you two on the beach. And if they didn't, they're probably watching the video now."

"Video?" she squeaked. Oh no. Not a sex tape. She was no better than James, getting caught in the act.

"Simmo and me, we thought we'd witnessed a rape, so we gave the video to the hotel manager as evidence." He glanced at her. "When you said you were meeting your boyfriend up here, I thought you were just being shy. Turns out he's a bit more than your boyfriend, isn't he? How much did he pay for you at auction, Miss Chastity?"

Flavia's voice died in her throat. Not only did he have a video of her naked with Jay, but he knew about the auction. She had to get out of here. Now. Flavia reached for the door just as someone shouldered through it from the other side, almost knocking her flat.

Relief flooded through Flavia at the sight of the hotel manager. "I need to get home. Off the island, I mean, and back to the airport," Flavia blurted out. "I have a flight to catch in the morning."

"I bet you do," Tim said, under his breath.

Flavia desperately prayed that the manager didn't hear him, or didn't care to ask him to elaborate.

"I hope you have travel insurance, then. None of us are leaving the island until Tuesday at the earliest. I'll see if we have a room I can give you for the weekend. I think there's a bed made up in the room in the staff accommodation, next to these guys." Ms Lane nodded at Tim.

"No!" Not next to the men who knew she'd sold her virginity and had the whole thing on film. "I'll pay for a hotel room. I can afford it."

Tim sniggered.

Ms Lane pursed her lips. "The resort's closed. All the hotel rooms, too. We sent all the linen back to the mainland for cleaning before we reopen next week. There's a spare bed in the staff accommodation, or there's Jay's villa. That's it. Seeing as you won't want to stay with Jay any more, that leaves —"

"Staying with Jay is fine," Flavia interrupted.

The manager stared. "But didn't he…"

"Oh, she likes Mr Felix just fine," Tim chimed in. "You should have seen them getting along in the helicopter. Real friendly, both of them. She's not going to want to go back to work as a travel agent in York after this weekend. Right, Flavia?"

Her heart plummeted. Oh God. Not only did he know about the auction, but while they were talking on the plane, she'd told him far too much. She had to get away from him. "Yes. I'll stay with Jay. I'll be fine."

The manager didn't want to let her go, but after Flavia repeated her reassurances several times, she was finally free. Free to trot away to Jay's villa, with her reputation in tatters. What would her family do when they found out what she'd done?

TWENTY-SIX

Someone tapped on the glass front door, jerking Jason out of the story he was reading. He marked his place with a crumpled envelope and stashed the book behind the couch cushions. He levered himself up, wincing as bits of him hurt. Jumping out of the helicopter probably hadn't been the best idea. Maybe he should wait a while before trying it again.

More tapping, barely audible over the slap of his bare feet on the tiles. Perhaps the tapper didn't want to be heard. It sure wasn't Xan, then. She'd have been shouting through the door by now.

"Yes?" he drawled as he waved open the automatic door. He allowed himself a smug grin at the sight of Miss Chastity's widening eyes. So she'd decided to accept his dinner invitation, after all.

"The helicopter's broken so I can't leave and I need

somewhere to stay. Ms Lane said the hotel's closed, so I have to stay here as your guest until I can get off the island." She said it all in a rush, like she was scared of being interrupted.

"Bullshit. Xan does her best to keep girls away from me. She didn't send you." Jason folded his arms across his chest, watching the inevitable way her gaze dropped from his face to his muscles. "You can do better than that, baby."

She reddened. "There was a cameraman. He said he got pictures of us on the beach!"

Jason shrugged. There was always some reporter or photographer or a dozen nosy nobodies with cameras on their phones. "Ask me nicely, baby. What was it you wanted? To be my guest until you get off again?"

"I…"

She was so nervous it took her a minute to understand the innuendo. Gah! Virgins.

She swallowed. "Can I please stay with you?"

"Sure, baby." Jason moved aside to let her past. He jerked his head toward the passage. "Bedroom's that way."

"I'll just go stash my stuff. I'll be right back," she said, not meeting his eyes.

Interesting. In the helicopter, she'd been as uninhibited as he could want, but now, after they'd done the deed, she was back to the shy girl who'd first climbed his steps with Xan only a few hours earlier. She had her money now. Maybe that was it. But she'd also had a taste of the things he could do to her delicious body. And no girl could resist that.

No more reading romance novels while she was here, or anything else that clashed with his rock god image. That wouldn't be hard with a pretty girl to seduce. Just like in the books. He had to sweep her off her feet completely, to make sure her first would be her only.

Just as long as she hadn't been pretending her enjoyment today. Pretending like Phuong...

Jason shook himself. This was different. This girl was a virgin, or she had been until they'd gotten hot and heavy in the helicopter. She wasn't married, she hadn't killed anyone, and he'd picked her, not the other way 'round. She couldn't have known he'd bid on her auction, let alone win it. And hadn't she said in the helicopter that she'd never intended to go through with it, until she saw him and couldn't say no? He was still a rock god – and she'd fallen under his spell. He just had to weave it a bit more...magically. Or something like that. He itched to grab one of the romance books hidden under the couch to see if there were any suggestions in there he needed to be reminded about, but she could return at any minute, so he ticked the points off in his head instead.

Exotic location: check.

Champagne: check.

Hotel room to themselves: check.

No phone calls to interrupt them: check.

A fancy dinner to seduce her over: well, he'd check that as soon as she returned and told him what she wanted.

Besides him, of course.

He wouldn't need any book after all that. He could play her body like a guitar, so well that she'd be begging for an encore.

"Hey, what do you want to order for dinner? I'm getting room service, baby," he called.

She emerged, her expression as cloudy as the sky outside. "Stop calling me that."

"My dear Miss Chastity, " Jason favoured her with an extravagantly low bow. "Would you do me the honour of informing me of your culinary preferences for our evening repast so that I may —"

"And that, too. I'm not your baby and I'm not chaste. Not any more. And if I forget, I'll have the whole experience on video to remind me." The girl whose name he didn't know slumped onto his couch.

Jason snorted. "It wasn't a very good video. Grainy as shit. They didn't even get the whole thing. Just the bit where I fell on top of you. You can't see your tits or anything. Now, if they'd been spying on us in the helicopter, they could have gotten some really steamy stuff."

She paled until her face was lighter than the couch. "Oh God."

"Nah, just call me Jay." He grinned, but she didn't seem to get the joke, so he decided to ask her again. "What do you want for dinner? There's only one chef on duty, so we have to get our order in."

"I don't care. Whatever."

Jason didn't really care what he ate, either. It was the dessert sitting on his couch he was interested in. He called room service, told the chef to bring a romantic dinner for two, and left it at that. Let the chef make decisions like steak or prawns or whatever.

He stretched out on the other couch, regarding the girl. "So, what do you want to do for the next hour while we wait for dinner?"

"Pretend none of this happened." At least that's what Jason thought she said. It was muffled by the cushion she'd buried her face in.

"We can pretend this is your first time all over again, if you like." He coughed out a laugh. "Just with a bit more space, a more comfortable seat and no helicopter."

"It's not the sex!" she snapped. "It's the cameras! What if it ends up on the news?"

Jason shrugged. "Wouldn't be the first time. Won't be the last, either, I bet. Part of being a public figure. You should be used to it. You've been all over the news for weeks with your auction. I bet there isn't an adult in Australia who hasn't heard of you. As for me, well…the media love sex stories about me. Especially when I do it in public. The only thing they'd like more is if I got arrested." There was a sour taste in his mouth at that. Xan and Shou had talked about bringing the police in. Good thing the helicopter had busted the satellite dish, then. No one could call the police and there was nowhere for their helicopter to land with Shou's broken bird on the pad. Now he had the whole long weekend to make this girl forget his unfortunate fainting fit. A four-day sex marathon seemed like an ideal distraction. He'd enjoy it, but so would she. He'd make certain of that. Jason stared up at the ceiling, dreamily considering all the things they could do together in four days. "Do you like chocolate?" he asked.

"Oh God, I feel sick," she moaned. "I'll never live this down."

Jason snorted. "Stop making such a big deal out of it. It's not a big deal, I promise you. The naked pictures of the Duchess of Cambridge on holiday lasted only a week in the news before everyone forgot about them. Yeah, you were naked, but no one can see anything. Not even your tits, I told you. You'll get five minutes of fame and then they'll forget about you."

Just like they'd forgotten about him while he'd been hiding out on the island. Not for much longer, though. He could see the headlines now: ROCK STAR BUYS GIRL'S VIRGINITY AT AUCTION.

"The news might, but no one else will. My family and friends will all know that I sold myself for sex. That I'm a prostitute." She sniffled and stared balefully at him with tear-reddened eyed. "And that you bought me."

Jason waved her worries away. "Nah, I didn't buy you. Or pay for sex, either. I only bought your virginity. Something you didn't even want any more. I don't need to pay for sex, baby."

"Stop calling me baby!" She jumped to her feet. "My name's Flavia. Seeing as the whole world will know soon enough, you may as well know. My name's Flavia and I'm a travel agent from York. There. Now you know."

"Flavia." He tasted her name, liking the exotic sound of it. "Flavia, with the salt-flavoured pussy, who seduced a rock star in a helicopter." He dropped his voice to a whisper. "We can do it all over again after dinner. All night, if you like. As long as I get to taste – "

"Stop. Just…stop. I feel sick. I'm not hungry any more. I'm…I'm going to bed." She took two steps before she turned. "Alone." A few seconds later, Jason heard the door of the guest room shut.

Fuck. Flavia was as crazy as Phuong. Why did he keep ending up with crazy chicks?

Shaking his head, Jason lay back on the couch. Figuring Flavia out was more than he could manage tonight. So much for Good Friday. Instead of good shit happening, it had turned into an unmitigated disaster. Maybe tomorrow would improve his Easter. It had fucking better.

TWENTY-SEVEN

Try as she might, Flavia didn't sleep. Her starved stomach snarled at her for forgetting dinner, but she knew she couldn't keep anything down. Round and round her head ran the worry about what her family and friends would say when they found out. Chasing it was the memory of Jay shrugging the whole sex video off as no big deal. It might not be a big deal for him to be caught on camera with his clothes off – God knew she'd found enough pictures of his body online to fantasise about for the next decade – but she'd never live this down. She could lose her job, her friends…everything. She'd never be able to show her face in York again. She'd have to move to….London or Toronto or somewhere on the opposite side of the world to home and everyone and everything she'd ever known, so they could busily forget they'd ever known her.

At least she had the money to travel wherever she

wanted now. How ironic. She'd need it.

Some time in the early hours of the morning, when it was still dark but some hopeful birds had decided that maybe it wasn't quite dark enough to stay asleep, Flavia came to her own decision. She couldn't face Jay any more. When the sun rose, she'd sneak out of the house. She'd find the hotel manager and beg her to find her a way off the island, or at least hide her until she could escape. She fell into a light doze, waking to find sunlight streaming into the room through the gaps in the blinds. Time to go. Time to leave behind all thoughts of Jay and auctions and…

Flavia didn't want to think about what had happened between her and Jay in the helicopter, though the sweet ache between her thighs seemed intent on reminding her of everything he'd done to her body. Certainly more than she'd bargained for, though he'd definitely had her hearty consent at the time. How could she refuse him? The man was lust on legs. Every Aussie girl's fantasy. Even hers. Now if only she didn't associate the very sight of him with nausea at the thought of the video.

Damn it. Last night he'd seemed eager to repeat their…helicopter tryst, and she'd been so tempted to give in, but just the thought of the world knowing about what she and Jay had done in that sordid not-quite-sex tape had turned her desire to dust.

She couldn't stay with him. She'd feel cheap all over again and not enjoy a single minute of it. Not even when he…

Flavia forced herself to forget about the blissful things Jay did with her body as she yanked on some clothes. Scraping her hair back into a ponytail, she stared at her hollow-eyed reflection in the tiny mirror. She hadn't slept a wink and she wouldn't sleep at all until this whole mess was over. First step, getting the hell out of here. She shoved her belongings back into her suitcase and checked her watch. Quarter past seven. The manager might be awake. At least Jay wouldn't be. She'd heard him banging around the house for hours after she went to bed. It wasn't until well after midnight that he'd gone to bed or passed out on the couch or whatever rock stars did at the end of the day.

She carried her suitcase instead of wheeling it, hoping to make as little sound as possible so she wouldn't wake Jay if he was asleep on the couch. When she reached the sitting room, there was no sign of him, so she breathed a sigh of relief and dropped her heavy burden beside the door, ready to collect when she needed it.

The automatic door took her a few seconds to work out before she managed to wave it open. Palm trees and a perfect morning enticed her out, reminding her that Romance Island Resort was a paradise on Earth that only a select few got to see. She didn't want to think about the price she'd paid to be one of them. Much too high…but too late, now, too. Time for damage control and working out alternate travel arrangements, both things she was good at. Bye-bye to Miss Chastity the hooker; welcome back to Flavia the award-winning travel agent. Even the thought brought a tiny smile to her lips. She'd always wanted to see Europe and Canada, and travel agents could work anywhere. She'd miss everyone, though.

She found her way back to the staff canteen without seeing a single human being, but the clash of pans in the kitchen told her the cook was awake. Flavia considered asking him for directions to the manager's house, but she decided against it. It wasn't a huge island — surely the staff quarters would be close by. Figuring it was a good a choice as any, Flavia followed one of the paths she hadn't taken yesterday. Within minutes, the jungle parted to reveal parallel lines of prefabricated mining dongas — the staff accommodation, she assumed.

That was all well and good, but she'd seen bigger stables for Shetlands. The hotel manager surely wouldn't be housed in one of these. Perhaps if she continued, she'd come to the senior staff accommodation. Or, failing that, someone she could ask for directions. Surely everyone else on the island knew where the boss lived.

In the end, she didn't have to ask. The path ended at a deep, shady veranda with only three wide-spaced doors instead of the regimented six of each donga block. The doors bore signs: Head Chef, Security Chief and Hotel Manager. Bingo.

Flavia stepped over a pair of flippers and made her way through the piles of diving gear to the manager's door. She rapped her knuckles lightly on the laminate, then a second time, harder.

The knob clicked and turned before the door creaked open.

Flavia took a step back, confused.

Shou adjusted his boxer briefs, like he'd pulled them on in a hurry. "Can I help you?"

Oh God, had she interrupted the pilot and the hotel manager having sex? Flavia felt her face grow hot. "I just wanted to ask the manager when I'll be able to leave the island." Because it was the last place on Earth she wanted to be. Romance Island? The place should be called Lust Island.

"I'll tell her." Shou glanced inside. "It might be an hour or two before she gets back to you on that, though. We were in the middle of…breakfast when you arrived." He winked.

Thoughts of Jay talking about how she tasted danced through her mind, accompanied by remembered sensations of his tongue inside her. Inside this man's helicopter, for heaven's sake. Oh God, what if he knew about it?

"Yeah. Okay. See you later, then," Flavia mumbled, retreating.

She needed to change her name, move to another country and do something to change her appearance, too. Dye her hair. Start wearing glasses. Big, ugly ones that hid half her face. If that didn't work, she'd have to consider plastic surgery. That wouldn't come cheap, and from all she'd heard, it was bloody painful, too.

This was all James' fault. If he hadn't slept with that prostitute and ended up infamous across the internet, she'd be in Bali with the girls, gearing up for a wedding, instead of wishing she could hide for the next year. Maybe two. She'd booked plenty of gap year trips for people, wanting to work in London as bartenders for a few months in between backpacking around Europe. Pouring drinks couldn't be too hard, and everyone loved an Aussie accent. Provided no one recognised her…

"You're up early."

Flavia froze. The last person she wanted to see right now was Tim the cameraman. "I have to go," she blurted out, quickening her step.

"No, wait! I need to ask you something. What would you do if I promised to keep your name out of the press?"

Had he read her roiling mind? Flavia forced herself to stop. If her family never found out... "Anything. I'd do anything." What did she have to lose?

Tim grinned. "Well, it's like this. When we thought the video was evidence of a crime, we figured the police would get it and that's about it. Now we know there's more to the story, it's worth a whole lot of money to the right media. And it's worth a whole lot more if we can add an exclusive interview with the girl in the video. Maybe even enough to fund the first few seasons of our series. What do you say, Flavia? One little interview, just one tiny hour of your time, and no one will ever know who you are, or should I just sell the story to the highest bidder, along with everything I know?"

Flavia swallowed. If her family and friends never had to know what she'd done...

TWENTY-EIGHT

Xan tore her eyes away from the swimming rock star. Why did he have to swim past her kitchen window at the same time every morning, wearing nothing but a cheeky grin? "Who was it?"

Shou ambled into the kitchen. He uncapped her jar of instant coffee and took a suspicious sniff before he spooned some into a mug.

"Shou, who was at the door?"

"Mr Felix's latest girl. Seems she's had her fill of him, too." He tipped the contents of the kettle into his mug. "She said she'd speak to you later about it. Before I could say anything, she took off."

Xan's gut clenched. What had Jay done overnight? Nothing to mar that undeserved perfect body on display outside her window, evidently, but Flavia had seemed almost eager to spend last night with him. If this morning she'd changed her mind again… Xan kneaded her aching forehead. She couldn't keep up with the rock star or his…whatever Flavia was. Paid companion, perhaps?

"I better go see what she wants," Xan said, heading for the door. She paused to add, "If you want more than coffee, breakfast's served at seven in the staff dining room. You may as well leave your linen where it is in case I can't raise anyone on the radio to come get you. I still think you'd sleep more comfortably in one of the staff bedrooms instead of on my lumpy couch."

"But then I might miss out on joining you on your morning swim."

Xan forced herself not to look at the lagoon. "Yeah, I won't be going for a swim until a bit later." No way in hell was she sharing the lagoon with a naked rock star. Especially not when she was wearing a dive mask that let her see everything. She wanted to see fish, not his dangly bits.

Ugh. But first she needed to see about Flavia. If she wasn't dealing with one Jay Felix mess, it was another, Xan fumed as she marched out the front door.

The girl hadn't gotten far. She'd been bailed up by one of the film crew. The talkative one, Tim.

Xan caught the words *interview, video* and *sell*. All three combined were enough for her to forget Jay Felix to focus on an even bigger wanker than the rock star. "You even attempt to sell resort property and I'll have you arrested for theft, then sued for damages!"

The cameraman stared at her. "What are you talking about? I haven't stolen anything." Between his mild surprise and casual stance, Xan saw red.

"Every frame of footage you take on this private island belongs to Romance Island Resort. Any attempt to sell or otherwise transfer resort property is theft. That includes data in any form." Xan stopped so close to Tim, she could see the sweat beading his forehead. "The moment you set foot on this island, your confidentiality clause kicked in. You talk to the press and you'll be in breach of contract." Some days, Xan truly loved her job. She dropped her voice to a whisper. "You do that and not only will you not get paid for this job, but I'll be forced to invoice you for your use of resort property. The flights, the accommodation, the helicopter charter I'll arrange to have you removed from the island…do you know how much it costs to stay at Romance Island Resort?"

"Eight hundred dollars a night for their standard room. More during peak season and long weekends," Flavia piped up.

How in hell did she know that? Xan wondered, then remembered that Flavia was a travel agent. One who'd clearly done her research before coming here.

Xan recovered quickly. Her tone was cool as she continued, "I trust that your team will act like the professionals you are, and fulfil your contract to the letter without any more…unfortunate incidents. Especially ones I'd have to refer to the resort's legal team. You're here to film the island, not the guests. Are we clear?"

Tim looked like he wanted to argue. His mouth opened to make a mistake.

Xan knew the look well. She'd lost count of the number of backpackers who'd tried to argue their way out of every dollar of their expenses. Just like she had a thousand times before, she stared down the bloke who thought he could beat her until he realised he didn't stand a chance.

Tim mumbled an answer that Xan took as reluctant acquiescence. Then she watched him leave.

"What if he goes and emails someone now about everything that happened yesterday?" Flavia said, her voice barely above a whisper.

"The lawyers will have him. He'll be bankrupt before breakfast," Xan said loud enough for the retreating cameraman to hear. "Besides, like everything else here at the island, both the internet and phones are down until Tuesday. We're cut off from the world until then. The zombie apocalypse could happen on the mainland and we wouldn't even know."

Flavia didn't look particularly comforted by this. "I got the impression they really wanted the money for their business. If selling my story gets them more than you're paying, I don't think you'll stop them. By the time your lawyers get to them, the damage will already be done. Videos can go viral overnight and if anyone finds out that I —"

"Auctioned off your virginity to that wanker of a rock star?" Xan supplied.

Flavia's eyes widened and she backed away.

Xan sighed. "Nothing happens on this island that I don't know about. Running a celebrity resort isn't easy. The secrets I wish I didn't have to keep…but it's all part of the job, living here in paradise. We had to close the resort before I could book a film crew, and Jay bloody Felix fucked that up by inviting a guest."

"You talking about how good I am in bed?" Jay emerged

from the jungle, water trickling off everything. He had a towel, but he just dabbed at his chest with it, letting it dangle down just low enough to cover the essentials, without hiding the fact that he was still stark naked. Bloody exhibitionist.

Xan opened her mouth to shout at him, but she caught sight of Flavia's enraptured expression. The girl drank him in like ambrosia. She was addicted, all right. Xan's last suspicions of rape and violence melted away. Maybe the rock star really had fainted in the heat. Overexertion from being oversexed. That she could believe.

"With the film crew here, there's a high risk of a media leak. I caught one of them trying to persuade Flavia here to do an interview that they could sell to the press. I don't need to tell you how dangerous that would be to the resort's reputation." Xan fixed her eyes on Jay.

He shrugged. "So what? She'll just say what a hundred girls have before. That I'm awesome in bed."

Flavia flushed and stared at her feet.

Xan's exasperated breath hissed out through her teeth. "Fine, I guess I do need to explain it. I'm not talking about your reputation, but the resort's. The hotel you bought and pay me to keep in business. How long do you think we'll keep attracting high-profile guests if they think their secrets might make tomorrow's news? There's no point in this entire advertising campaign if we're painted as the exclusive resort that sells its guests' secrets to the highest bidder!"

"All right, all right! Calm down. What the fuck do we do?" For the first time, Jay looked like he actually cared about what she was about to say.

Xan tried not to look smug. "We let them do their job,

and you keep away from them. You both keep away from them." She sucked in a breath. "It might be best if you stayed in your villa as much as possible until they leave. I can't keep an eye on both of them every minute they're here, not with the GPS location link down. So no sex on the beach or any other public place where they might stumble across you. Can you at least keep the steamy stuff inside until Tuesday?"

Flavia turned an interesting shade of red.

Jay sported a predatory grin. "I'll try," he drawled, eyeing Flavia's discomfort. "But this girl is red-hot in the sack. If she wants me on the beach, I'm not one to refuse a lady." He slung his arm around Flavia's shoulders, where it left a damp trail. "C'mon, baby. Let's get you back to my place before you combust. I know a short cut through the jungle."

Xan watched the pair head down Jay's private path to Villa Penguin. She couldn't tail the camera crew all weekend, but she wouldn't have to. All she needed to ensure was that whatever photos and video they took never left the island. For that, she needed the cooperation of the IT boys, who had already volunteered to assist the film crew with their work for the weekend.

That meant starting work even earlier than usual. So much for a weekend off.

TWENTY-NINE

Flavia told herself she needed to break out of Jay's embrace, that it wasn't okay to walk around the island with his arm around her like they had a relationship instead of a business arrangement. Especially with the film crew roaming around. It would be incredibly easy, too, she told herself. All she had to do was shrug and his arm would slide off her shoulders. But it felt so good there. So…natural. Damn it, couldn't she just pretend for a few more minutes that she was the darling of Jay Felix, sex god? Yes. Yes, she could. Especially when the man wore nothing but a towel slung low around his hips.

Jay chuckled. "You checking me out, baby?"

Luckily, he didn't seem to need an answer.

"Hey, it's all yours, for the rest of the weekend, if you're feeling up to it."

"But…" Flavia's voice didn't seem to want to work, so

she cleared her throat and tried again. "But the contract. It said only once, and no contact afterwards. We did it once in the helicopter yesterday. That means…no more." She couldn't stop a small sigh of disappointment from escaping. How was she going to manage sharing a house with this man for the rest of the weekend without…more? But she couldn't have more. Once the weekend was over, she'd fly far away from this gorgeous man, never to see him again. She couldn't afford to lose her heart to him. That wasn't part of the contract.

"You mean the contract you tore up in the helicopter, before your first time? The one that's now null and void, seeing as you destroyed the document?"

Flavia stopped dead and Jay's arm slid off her, leaving her feeling oddly bereft. "But…" If the contract didn't exist, then all bets were off. All the rules could be broken and there was nothing she could do about it. Oh God, what if she gave in again and the next time was even more wonderful than lying in his arms in the helicopter? She wouldn't want to leave. Shit, she wouldn't want to even look at another man again.

"Don't look so scared, baby. With no contracts, we can make it up as we go. Breaking the rules will be so much fun, you'll see." With one wink, he made her wonder which rule he wanted to break first.

If she got a choice, she'd vote for breaking the no-kissing rule, because after his swim, she was certain his lips would be as salty as seawater. Would his tongue be cold, or as warm as when he'd slid it inside her yesterday? The rest of his skin was cool to the touch right now, drawing her attention every time he brushed against her as they continued walking.

They turned a corner and abruptly, the jungle ended on a paved path – the path that led to Jay's house. This time, Flavia was scared to enter. Not because she was nervous about what Jay might do to her body – with every passing moment, her body reminded her how good it felt when he touched her – but because when she left that house in a few short days, she'd be forced to give up the most addictive experience of her life. Quitting smoking would be easier than giving up Jay Felix.

But she could do this. She'd already given Jay Felix the rest of her body. But James had smashed her heart – and she couldn't face piecing together the jagged shards so it would be whole again for Jay. That made things simple: Jay Felix couldn't have her heart. With that thought firmly fixed in her mind, Flavia followed Jay up the steps into his villa.

Her bag stood sentinel just inside the door, reminding her that she didn't belong here. Grabbing the handle, she dragged it back to the guest room where she'd tossed and turned last night. Her room now. Maybe she should try to get some more sleep, now she knew the sex tape wouldn't be taking over the internet any time soon.

"I'm going to grab a shower. You're welcome to join me, if you want," Jay said.

Flavia shook her head, too tired to talk any more.

He shrugged, not looking put out at all. "I'd say watch whatever you like on TV, but all the channels are down with the satellite link out of action. If you're really bored, there are some books under the couch someone left here. I keep meaning to take them back to the resort library, but I never seem to get around to it. Take your pick."

A book might take her mind off things enough to help her drift off to sleep, Flavia mused, waiting for Jay to tramp off to the bathroom before she checked under the couch. When she did, she was surprised to see two neat stacks of paperbacks. She reached for the first stack and almost choked with laughter at the cover of the book on top. She'd expected thrillers, but the first one had a naked male torso on the front (not unlike Jay's, come to think of it) and the back cover copy proclaimed that it was a rock star romance. One of Jay's previous partners had been a fan of rock star romance? It was just too funny.

Deciding that rock stars would only make temptation worse, she examined the other books. Every single one was a romance of one kind or another, with the majority of them rock star romances. Whoever the mystery girl was, she'd definitely liked her rockers. Why, then, wasn't she with Jay now, if she liked men like him so much?

Setting the rock stars aside, Flavia found she was left with a small stack of stories about mail-order brides. Now that was a weird thing to find under a rock star's couch. The rock star romances made sense, seeing as any girl who read those would jump at the chance to live the fantasy with a man like Jay, but mail-order brides and rock stars made no sense. That probably meant they'd belonged to two different girls. The mail-order marriage fangirl wouldn't have lasted long with Jay, a man more for one night stands than marriage. Mail-order brides were for lonely farmers and station owners who barely saw women outside of their infrequent trips into town and, of course, the annual Bachelor and Spinsters' Ball. There were talks of York hosting it next year, though she didn't think it likely. If the unlikely happened, she'd be there in a heartbeat, if only to say she'd been to a B&S.

But that was all immaterial at the moment. Now, her choices were between rock stars and mail-order brides. Thinking of Jay in the shower, Flavia reached for a rock star and settled on the couch with her book.

"Hey. Baby. Flaaaaavia. Are you hungry?"

What? Flavia levered her eyes open and found Jay's face so close she could barely focus on it. She shoved herself upright, her eyes darting around the room in an effort to orient herself. She sat on the couch in Jay's villa. He was perched on the coffee table, beside a basket she hadn't seen before.

"The book's that good, huh? I never understand why chicks read romance books. I mean, I'm right here. Isn't the real thing better?" Jay sighed. "Yet I find you cheating on me with a fictional character. Sleeping with a book about —" He twisted his head to read the cover. " – some rock star who falls for the nanny? Hang on, you're not a nanny, are you? Do you take care of kids for a living?"

Flavia swallowed, trying to moisten her dry throat. She needed a drink. Water would be nice, but she wouldn't say no to alcohol right now. "No. Not usually, anyway. I'm a travel agent. The most I deal with kids is when our office has to arrange a high school exchange trip."

Jay stretched out on the other sofa. "So, you spend all your spare time travelling? Is that what you need the money for?"

"I didn't need the money," Flavia snapped. "That's not what the auction was about at all."

Jay's eyes smouldered. "Enlighten me."

Flavia hesitated. Hell, she thought about not answering at all, but who could she tell? Not Violet. Not any of her other friends. Not her family. No one else would understand. Just...Jay. Before she'd even decided she wanted to, she found herself pouring out the whole story about James and the buck's night sex tape. Tears fell like rain when she described how worthless she felt at being told so many lies when she'd done everything for him, and he'd thrown it all away mere weeks before their wedding. And the media storm around the auction...at first, she'd felt a bit of pride at the price they'd attached to her, the Million Dollar Girl and all, but after a while, her satisfaction waned as people took to social media and then the reporters filled their articles with the most malicious comments they could find. She'd even started avoiding the auction site, because of all the rude questions people had left that she refused to answer. Most of them had suggested the reason she'd never had sex was because there was something wrong with her, and they wanted to know what. "They never thought I might be saving myself for someone, because I chose to do it. Not because I couldn't, or I didn't want to," she finished, reaching for a tissue to mop her eyes.

She realised she'd been talking without cease for a long time and Jay hadn't said a word for a while. Oh God, had she bored him into oblivion?

No, Jay's eyes were wide open and...curious?

"I don't get it. You say you don't need the money, that your life was just fine except for some cheating wanker, but you thought you'd sell yourself to feel like a million dollars?"

Oh God. Flavia's eyes brimmed with tears again. "It

wasn't perfect. My life revolved around James and the wedding, and all of a sudden…"

Understanding lit Jay's eyes. "You felt worthless. Like everything you'd worked for, all your hopes and dreams, were crushed into nothingness because of a stupid decision someone else made." He gritted his teeth. "So you wanted the best revenge, where you can show them how stupid their choices are by making them regret what they've lost."

Now it was Flavia's turn to stare. How could Jay possibly understand her so perfectly? A rock god like him could hardly have known any failure in his life, let alone loss. His band had broken up at the pinnacle of their careers, with more money and fame than anyone their age had a right to. And yet…and yet…somehow this rock star could see straight into her heart. "Yes."

"You know what's better than that, though?" he went on. "It's when things stop being about revenge and more about your own happiness. Their lives are their own to fuck up, but you can do whatever you like with yours. Do what makes you happy, and losers who don't like it can fuck off." He winked. "How'd you like to find out what happiness feels like with me?"

Her mouth dropped open. "All that stuff about feelings and revenge and happiness was just so you could ask me to have sex with you?" She'd been such an idiot to believe that this shallow bastard understood what feelings were.

To her surprise, Jay burst out laughing. "Fuck, I don't need pick-up lines or psychology to get into a girl's pants. When I want a girl, I tell her I can give her the best night of her life, full of sex that will spoil her for anyone else. I don't get turned down very often."

Flavia tried to keep her face blank, so she could hide the rising warmth within her, reminding her of exactly what Jay meant by the best night of her life. She'd never forget that night in the helicopter. He'd definitely ruined her for anyone else…because how could she ever want anyone else, after one night with Jay Felix?

Jay bounced onto the sofa beside her. "So, what do you say, baby?"

No wasn't an option, but no sound seemed to want to come out of her mouth.

His voice dropped to a honeyed purr. "Are you hungry, baby?"

Her gaze dropped to his groin. Through the folds of his shorts, it was hard to tell if he was aroused or not. Not that it mattered. Jay wasn't the sort of man to ever experience a failure to launch.

"Because I have something special for you." Jay reached for the basket. Confused, Flavia watched him withdraw package after package, until everything was spread out like a picnic on the table. "I asked the chef for his romantic picnic for two pack. It's best eaten on a blanket on the beach, but seeing as you want to stay here, I figured I'd lay it all out on the table for you."

Flavia tried to shake the half-formed fantasies from her lust-filled brain. Lunch. He'd been talking about lunch. And now he was…yes, he was laughing at her. "I'm sorry. I'm still half asleep," she offered in excuse, but she knew Jay saw through her.

"We can play by the rules on your ripped-up pages, or we can play the way I do things best. Live and unplugged and improvised, fuelled by passion alone." Jay nodded at the table. "Lunch now, and I've made arrangements for dinner later. No, I didn't order for you. I didn't even order for me — I told the chef to make something good. If we don't like it, we can send it back and order something else. And go with whatever feels right, baby."

Somehow, she got stuck in his honey eyes. Though her stomach grumbled for her attention, all she could think about was the joy of sex with Jay.

"So what do you say, Flavia? Your way, with rules and contracts and no fun, or mine, where we do what we like? I have some ideas about what I'd like to do with you tonight, and I think you'll enjoy them even more than last night."

A warm hand stopped her from pulling her shirt off.

"Not yet, baby. It's lunchtime. Time for food, not sex. I'll give you what you want, but not for a while. Not until you're so ready for it, you're begging for release."

Staring into his eyes, Flavia wanted to believe him with her whole being. Even her traitorous heart wanted a bit of this action. With her last smidgin of self-control, she swore that was the one part of her he couldn't have. Her whole body was his to play with as he pleased, she thought with a thrill, but her heart was her own. Nobody's plaything. At least, she hoped so.

THIRTY

Jason breathed a sigh of relief as he reclined on the couch. Crisis averted. He still wasn't sure how he'd managed to fuck up last night, but this morning everything seemed rosy with Flavia again and he didn't want to jeopardise that. He'd go full-throttle romance until there wasn't a hint of doubt in her eyes, then he'd draw it out until after eight. THEN he'd have the rest of the night to make her abso-fucking-lutely certain there was no one better for her than him, and she wouldn't even be able to recall the name of that James arsehole. Maybe he'd even manage to get Phuong out of his head, too. He'd do his damn best to forget her, anyway, as he spent all night loving every inch of Flavia's untouched body. He had to give her multiple orgasms every time or he just wouldn't live up to the hype. All the heroes in the library's romance books did, and he wasn't going to fall short of some Fabio-like fucker. He figured he might've had an excuse in the helicopter last night, what with the limited time, cramped quarters and him fainting, then jumping out of the helicopter and all, but that definitely didn't excuse him now.

By the time he was done with Flavia, she wouldn't even remember her own fucking name, because she'd be too busy screaming his. Fuck yeah.

Ignoring the twin siren calls from his cock and her bedroom eyes, Jason grabbed one of the Turkish bread things from the basket and bit into it. At least the resort had a decent chef. Some tours he'd been on, they couldn't even get a decent Chiko roll backstage. He remembered at one concert, there'd been waiters serving champagne and caviar. To rock stars. Who the fuck actually liked champagne and caviar? He'd always been a beer and bourbon man. Wine had been something he only drank if he was desperate and they couldn't afford anything else, and that wasn't from a glass. Fuck, no. If you didn't guzzle it straight from the goon bag, you weren't fucking doing it right. He bet Flavia had never done that. Drunk on goon, she'd never have stayed a virgin. Even he hadn't, gawky kid that he'd been. He couldn't even remember the name of the first girl he'd slept with. He'd never had the guts to ask a girl for sex until that night, slosh-full of cheap wine, when she'd asked him if he knew what a reverse cowgirl was, and if he didn't, whether he'd like her to show him.

Fuck. That'd been a long time ago. Maybe he should try introducing Flavia to it later. She was from a farm, wasn't she? Cowgirl might be just her style. He had plenty of time to find that out.

He finished his half of lunch quickly, then excused

himself and left while Flavia's mouth was too full to speak. Now he'd seen which items she'd chosen to eat, he could report back to the chef with some ideas for dinner. He wasn't stupid enough to order food for a girl when he didn't know what they liked – he knew that was the fastest way to fuck up a first date. Any bloke who did that was just asking to get his arse kicked by his date's deceptively delicate high heels. At least, that's what his sister said, and Jo's advice on women had served him well until now. For a second, he wished he could call Jo now, to make sure she approved of his plans for Flavia, but even if the phones had been working, Jo was with Mum and Dad this weekend, and he didn't fancy them finding out what he was up to. The auction aspect probably wouldn't go down too well with any of them, either.

Nah, he should just focus on Flavia and giving her a weekend so awesome she'd never want to leave. He had to make up for messing up her first night in paradise. Maybe he should make a few changes to the menu tonight, to make everything that bit more memorable. In fact...

He marched to the kitchen, his mind full of ideas on how to make Flavia's evening perfect. Even before her clothes came off. He could do romance. He'd been reading about it for weeks. Rock stars in books had drug and alcohol issues, came from fucked-up families or were complete arseholes, yet they managed romance. How hard could it be?

THIRTY-ONE

"And he wanted me to match wine with every course. Do I look like a wine waiter? All served on a table that has to be set up exactly to his specifications. As if that wasn't enough, then he came back with another set of demands, including precise times for the courses. That wasn't the worst of it. Instead of the dessert I've already prepared, he wants bombe Alaska. One of the most difficult desserts to make in a tropical climate, between keeping things frozen and keeping the meringue just the right consistency, but it has to be served at precisely 7.30 pm on that jetty – the same time as dinner is served in the staff dining room. So he expects me to leave the kitchen and my own dinner, to cart over his dessert and set fire to it while he's sitting on a structure made entirely of wood. At low tide. You know what else he asked for? I should say demanded. He…"

Xan nodded drowsily as Patel continued to rant, making

a mental note never to give the man sole control of the kitchen again. And she'd thought Jay Felix was a prima donna. Patel truly took the cake — or he would, if he shut up long enough to make it first.

Speaking of shutting up, it looked like he was finally winding down.

"Do you have the ingredients, and can you prepare everything in time for dinner?" Xan interjected.

Patel hesitated. Probably loath to stop his ranting to answer questions, Xan thought.

"Perhaps," he ventured. "But — "

Xan held up her hand. "I'll see if I can get Jackie to serve. You just take care of the cooking. If anything can't be done because you don't have the time or ingredients, or it's just not safe, tell Jay and offer him a suitable alternative."

Patel opened his mutinous mouth to argue.

Xan cut him off. "I realise he's making extra work for you, but he's the owner. He gets treated the same way as any other celebrity staying in the Pearl Villas." She experienced a twinge of guilt as she said it, but she ignored it and continued, "He's trying to impress a travel agent. I assume you've heard that the resort is doing a big PR push? With new television ads, so we've closed the resort for a week to let a camera crew come and film the island. Think of this dinner as another PR exercise. Imagine she's the food editor for *The West*. If we show her the resort at its best, she'll go back to her office and rave about us. But if we mess it up, she might not mention us at all, or, if she does, it'll only be to say what a horrible experience she had here. Look, I know Jay Felix isn't the easiest man to get along with, but one thing he's amazing at is building an image that millions drool over. He lives and breathes public relations because media attention is what made him a star. If he says to build a bomb…then you pull out all the stops and build him a bomb."

"Bombe Alaska, not a bomb," Patel grumbled, but his expression had softened. Perhaps it was more accurate to say it didn't look like he was likely to explode any more, unless Jay sparked his short fuse again.

Xan wouldn't put it past him, but after seeing the look on that girl's face this morning when she saw Jay, especially after yesterday's fiasco, she decided to give the man a break. He had a way with women – one which didn't extend to her, but then he wasn't her type, so that didn't matter – that turned them into adoring fangirls. If he truly wanted to make up for messing up Flavia's first time, then perhaps she should give him the chance.

"Right," she replied absently. "So you do your best to put together that romantic dinner, and I'll go back to…whatever I was doing." She waited for Patel to disappear from view before she headed for the library.

It was supposed to be her day off, damn it, and she intended to spend at least some of it relaxing. Xan scanned the shelves, but the library was surprisingly light on murder mysteries. Not that she minded. Not really. Give her a good romance any day and she was happy. Speaking of romances…once again, she searched for the book she'd been reading in the pub a few weeks back, but it was nowhere to be found. Damn it, she really wanted to know how it ended. She still couldn't work out how a virginity auction could end in happily ever after for the couple…though Jay and Flavia looked like they were well on their way to something like that this morning.

Xan shook her head. Just the thought of the financial transaction for flesh left a bad taste in her mouth. Was it because she was English? Old-fashioned? Religious she wasn't, seeing as she'd grown up knowing all the stories of the Greco-Roman pantheon, which had taught her that deities did the stupidest things, divine or not.

"Ms Lane?"

Xan whirled and found herself face to face with Simon. "Yes?"

"We took advantage of the weather and captured as much of the island as we could while the sun shone. We think it's pretty much a wrap. Your IT guys have been very helpful. Once our memory cards were full, we just handed them over and they took care of downloads and backup so we could keep filming." Simon cleared his throat. "The only thing left to do is some nightscapes. Tim said something about tonight's moonrise?"

Xan nodded. "The best view of moonrise is from the eastern beaches at low tide. That's around eight tonight." Once a dive master, always a dive master – Xan knew the tides and moon phases wherever she worked. The best times for snorkelling, the best times for diving and even the best times for fishing. With the fourteen-metre tides up here, almost every schedule on the island revolved around tides. Especially the one for the supply boat. Which reminded her – she needed to radio the pearl farm again, to see when they'd be able to get a boat out, or better yet, whether they'd managed to contact a repairman with the parts to fix the helicopter and the satellite dish.

She wouldn't hold her breath. The Easter long weekend

was hardly the time for miracles to happen.

THIRTY-TWO

"How would you like a walk on the beach?"

Flavia raised her eyes from her book. "I thought we were supposed to stay inside."

Jay shrugged. "What the point of living in paradise if you don't go outside to enjoy it? C'mon. I'll fend off the wildlife."

What sort of wildlife did this island have that required fending off? Flavia hadn't seen anything larger than a lorikeet and she was certainly a match for one of those.

Jay flashed a smile that would make any girl swoon. "Please?"

Forgetting her book, Flavia rose, ready to…what had he asked her to do again? She took his outstretched hand and followed him through the front door and down the steps to the sand. A jetty stuck out into the sea, or it would have if the sea hadn't retreated. Instead, it stood high above a smooth stretch of sand. The sun had sunk below the palm trees, but she could still feel its warmth in the boards that had gorged on the sun's rays all day.

Jay let go of her hand and swung onto a ladder fixed to the side of the jetty. "Down here." He climbed out of sight.

Flavia felt a flutter of nerves in her tummy, then realised that it was probably just hunger. Lunch had been a long time ago and dinner…well, she'd have to ask Jay about that. She wasn't the best cook most days, and Jay had mentioned a chef. She didn't want to be caught in Jay's kitchen when the professional arrived. He'd either shout at her for her incompetence or laugh himself sick.

"Come on! Or do you want me to throw you over my shoulder and carry you down here?" Jay called from below.

He must think her some sort of stupid city girl who'd never climbed a ladder in her life. Just because she'd never had sex before him, didn't make her completely inexperienced. The rungs vibrated like lightly struck bells under her hands and feet, sounding her arrival. Her feet sank deep into damp sand at the bottom, surprisingly cool after the warm rungs.

"Guess not, then. This way." Jay beckoned and she followed, both leaving footprints that pooled with water on the pristine sand to mark their path.

Flavia rounded a clump of palm trees and stumbled to a halt. Someone had set out a line of tiny tea light candles, flickering in the light evening breeze in the shape of a – she walked closer to get a better look – heart, ringing a white-skirted table set for two. A romantic dinner on the beach? With Jay? Flavia couldn't take her eyes off the table. Why would he…

"I thought you might like a little romance with your dinner. I wanted to arrange something special for you when you first arrived but yesterday…wasn't a normal day by anyone's standards, even mine. I got a bit side-tracked." A sheepish grin surfaced that reminded Flavia of no sheep she'd ever seen. If she had, she'd never wonder where all the sheep jokes came from. Any sheep that grinned like that would be irresistible.

Sheep. She was thinking about sheep when she had Jay Felix in front of her.

"This is how you romance girls?" Her voice sounded hoarse.

Jay laughed. "Not usually. Ask the chef, if you don't believe me. I think he wanted to tell me to shove my candles up my arse."

Flavia forced a smile. "Kinky." Her heart froze. Was that what Jay had in mind? Getting her to lower her guard so he could persuade her to do the sort of kinky stuff that he did with other girls? No. Just…no.

"Not my style. And the chef isn't my type, either." Jay winked. "You, though…are exactly my type."

Her breath caught in her throat.

"Sweet. Pretty. Not a pushover — not afraid to take charge, if that first time on the beach was any indication. And not too shy to enjoy yourself." Jay ran his hands through his hair. "Fuck, you were hot in that helicopter. I can't stop thinking about it. About how I'd like to do it all over again, and show you more pleasure than you've ever dreamed of."

She felt like her eyes were so wide, they'd pop out of their sockets. Jay Felix wanted to spend more time with her? He'd been thinking about her as much as she'd dreamed about him?

Jay clapped his hands, startling her out of her reverie. "But sex can wait. Now, I'd like to take you to dinner."

For the second time that evening, she took his hand and allowed him to lead her – this time, to her seat.

Jay took his place across from her. Glass clunked against metal as he withdrew a dripping bottle from an ice bucket, half-hidden in the tablecloth's folds. "Wine?" he offered, popping the cork free.

No wine expert, Flavia didn't even glance at the label. It had bubbles and alcohol, both of which were probably a bad idea in her unsettled stomach, but if it calmed her nerves at all, it would be worth it.

Jay filled her flute, then his own, and raised his in a toast. "To following your heart."

That was a strange thing to drink to. Flavia clinked her glass against his before she drank deeply. The cold, dry fizz went straight to her head, freezing her brain into tipsiness. Probably a good thing. She wouldn't worry so much now – maybe she'd even be able to enjoy this dinner. It's not like she'd ever share a meal with a rock star again after this weekend.

A woman with a laden tray appeared, laying plates on the table.

"Thanks, Jackie," Jay said, and Jackie left.

Flavia peered at her tiny, manicured salad, outlined in yet another heart made from two king prawns. She knew girls who'd consider such a salad a complete meal, but growing up on a sheep farm had given her different ideas. Surely this snack wouldn't be enough to satisfy Jay?

"I thought you liked prawns. You ate all the ones at lunch." Jay snapped the head off one of his and tossed it in a bowl presumably placed to catch the crustacean carcass.

So he was teasing her with a tiny meal because she ate all the prawns? Fine. She wouldn't give him the satisfaction of a response. Instead, she peeled her prawns, sliced them into smaller pieces that she sprinkled liberally over the lettuce, and started eating her salad.

Five forkfuls and her plate was empty. Flavia down set her fork and gulped her wine until the glass was empty.

"More?" a female voice asked.

Flavia stared at Jackie, then recovered and nodded. Jackie lifted the bottle from the ice and refilled both of their glasses. The efficient woman replaced their empty plates with new ones, bracketing the steaming dishes with clean cutlery.

A small morsel of fish sat in a pool of sauce, with what looked like strands of seaweed on top. Flavia had seen bigger pieces of sushi.

Jay scooped the whole thing off his plate and shovelled it into his mouth. Trying not to laugh at his bulging cheeks, she sliced hers in half and managed to finish her fish in two decorous bites. It was a lovely taste, but she could have eaten the whole fillet, not a spoonful of it.

"Hey, Jackie," Jay called. "How many courses after this one? I gave the chef a schedule. This is the last night. I don't want it messed up."

Flavia's heart sank. Somewhere in her head she knew she could never keep Jay, but to hear him state so baldly that he didn't want to see her after tonight…hurt. Like a slap in the face.

She drank some more wine, hoping to dissolve the lump that had risen in her throat, but that only seemed to make it worse. Tears threatened and she blinked furiously to banish them. Jay didn't deserve to see her cry if he was only going to dismiss her in the morning. In fact, he didn't deserve anything else from her, at all. It's not like the contract allowed him anything after the first time. She'd finish her dinner, grab her romance book, then shut herself in her room and read until she fell asleep. Alone. Jay Felix could go fuck himself for all she cared: he couldn't have her again.

Jackie switched the plates again. Flavia squinted at this new offering, wondering if the meat at the bottom of the carefully constructed edifice was beef or pork. It didn't matter much, anyway, she decided, using her knife and fork to cut a sliver to taste.

It was neither. She tasted fresh lamb, as fresh as she got at home at the right time of year. How had Jay or the chef gotten their hands on a lamb that couldn't have been slaughtered more than a day or two ago? Was there a paddock hidden among the palm trees that she'd missed?

Jay hadn't missed her expression. "Good, isn't it? We get all our meat fresh from the local sheep and cattle stations. Most of the Kimberley beef gets exported, but the resort's always had arrangements with the local people."

What did the animals eat up here? Back home, there were paddocks of grass and clover come winter and spring, and hay to do them through the summer and autumn until the rains came. Flavia hadn't seen any grass except for the occasional lawn in town. Definitely not when she'd flown up in the helicopter. Nothing but scrubby bushes and stunted trees. Unless they ate the scrub…

Damn it. He had her thinking about sheep again. Flavia focussed on her meal instead. This portion was bigger, and she started to feel full. Good thing the fish dishes hadn't been any bigger, or she wouldn't be able to fit this one in.

"More wine?"

Flavia found she'd emptied her glass again, so she agreed to allow Jackie pour her another before the woman took away her empty plate. This time, she didn't immediately replace it with another course, and Flavia was grateful for the reprieve. She wasn't sure she could eat any more tonight.

"So what did you think?" Jay asked, sipping his wine.

Flavia raised her eyes to the sky, wanting a moment to get the words right in her head before she lost all sense of reason in Jay's smouldering eyes. She was surprised to see stars already – night descended quickly out here. It seemed like only moments ago she'd been surrounded by a twilight edged with rust along the horizon, but now she only saw darkness pricked with light.

"It's all…wonderful," she said, and was rewarded with Jay's heart-stopping smile. His eyes glowed in the candlelight, like twin flames themselves. Lighting a fire inside her that she wasn't sure she could extinguish.

"Good," Jay replied. "Because the night isn't over yet." Now his eyes held promises.

Promises her heart prayed he'd keep, because despite her best efforts, she knew she was definitely in danger of losing her heart to this man.

THIRTY-THREE

"Your dessert." Jackie laid a platter on the table between them. In the dim candlelight, Jason thought it looked like a pair of boobs, complete with nipples on top. He frowned. He liked tits as much as any man, and he had plans that involved Flavia's later on tonight, but he hadn't ordered the pair perched on the plate now.

Jackie flicked a lighter and ignited something in her hand. Jason had taken it for a particularly large candle holder, but the leaping blue flame erupting from it put paid to that idea. Before he could ask what it was, she tipped the glass over the tits, haloing them in blue fire.

Flavia yelped and jumped back from the table, terrified of the flaming tits. "Why did you do that?"

"Bombe Alaska. You have to fire it to sear the meringue on the outside," Jackie replied patiently. She scooped one mound onto a plate and placed it in front of Flavia, before giving the other to Jason. "I'll go see to the rest of your instructions." She vanished into the darkness.

Flavia still stared at her plate as if she was afraid the flames would leap up and burn her.

Jason sucked in a breath and blew out the flames on his bombe. A wisp of smoke curled up toward the faint stars overhead, smelling of burnt sugar. He'd never had this before, so he didn't hesitate to dig his fork through the singed meringue to the ice cream and cake beneath. He stuck a big spoonful in his mouth and closed his eyes as it melted on his tongue. Heaven. He had to order this more often.

He glanced at Flavia, who hadn't touched hers. The alcohol had burned itself out, but the absence of flames didn't seem to reassure her one bit.

She wasn't used to much, Jason told himself. If she'd never had sex, maybe she'd never had a flaming dessert before, either. "It's meringue, cake and ice cream," he told her, spooning some more of his. "Here, taste it." He held out the loaded spoon.

Flavia hesitated for a moment, then leaned forward and opened her mouth. Jason slipped the spoon between her lips and was rewarded with her humming satisfaction. She swallowed, then said, "And passionfruit. Meringue, cake and ice cream with passionfruit pulp on top. Kind of like an inverted pavlova." Finally, she dug into her dessert.

Jason shrugged and returned to eating his own. So that's what the gooey, tart, seedy stuff was with the ice cream. It sort of worked.

All too soon, dessert was done and his watch told him it was time to move if he wanted to get the best view of moonrise.

Flavia had gobbled her dessert faster than he had, once she'd gotten over her initial fright. Now, she was scraping the last drops of melted ice cream from her plate, as if she couldn't get enough of it. Jason suppressed a snort. Fuck, she was so innocent. He wanted to show her the world, all of his world, and watch her as she viewed it with wide, new eyes, before embracing it with all the excitement she'd shown in the helicopter. Was it so wrong to want to share that with her?

Her spoon tinkled to the table. "If I eat any more, I'll explode," she declared.

Good. He had other things to show her, and Jason couldn't wait. "C'mon. I want you to see something."

He took her hand, guiding her between the candles in the sand, before breaking into a run. More candles guided them, lit by Jackie and her trusty lighter, no doubt, all the way back to the paved path to Villa Penguin. No ladders this time as Jason led Flavia back to the jetty by the proper path.

Flickering candles surrounded an ice bucket of wine at the end of the jetty, just as he'd asked. He led her along the boards, their footsteps thumping loudly in the velvety dark. His feet touched the picnic blanket Jackie had thoughtfully laid out and Jason made a mental note to thank the woman for her foresight.

He helped Flavia sit down, then dropped to the blanket beside her, offering her yet another glass of wine. The cork's explosive pop echoed in the darkness, before the familiar glugging of alcohol into a glass soothed Jason's nerves. He'd never done this romantic shit before. Not for anyone. He was as new to this as Flavia, but he couldn't afford to fuck it up.

They sipped in silence for a while. Jason fought to keep his breathing calm and even. He hadn't overdone the romance, had he? Was that why she was so quiet?

Not wanting to risk breaking the silence, he stared up at the stars. Faint lights against overwhelming darkness. He remembered hearing that the stars he saw today were just the memory of the brilliant balls of gas they once were, before they'd burned out, long in the past, and the faint light reaching him now was all that was left of them. Was he like them? Had Jay Felix the rock star burned out too brightly so that all that was left of him was a faint pinprick of light, to be seen by someone in the future who wouldn't even know his name, let alone his legacy? The light in Flavia's eyes when she looked at him said his star wasn't extinguished yet. His brightness hadn't burned out for her.

Was it so wrong to want her for more than the auction's allotted single time? She'd ripped up the contract, so she surely didn't still hold to its tenets. The girl had been betrayed by her fiancé, for fuck's sake. No wonder she didn't trust men any more. But she could trust him. He'd never do wrong by her. He'd make sure she loved every minute with him, from now until forever.

"What's that?" Flavia pointed at the horizon, where a faint orange smudge was visible over the ocean.

As they watched, it grew bigger and brighter, a glowing semicircle rising over the waves, which faintly reflected its brilliance.

"Must be the moonrise," Jason said, staring just as intently. He knew this happened every month, but he'd never watched the full moon rise over the tidal flats before. Fuck, it was awesome.

"It's beautiful," Flavia breathed, shifting closer so that her shoulder touched his.

Fuck it. He was never one to let an opportunity go to waste. Jason wrapped his arm around her and leaned in to break her stupid no-kissing rule.

THIRTY-FOUR

Jackie appeared in the dining room, conveying with a single nod that she'd accomplished her mission of serving Jay's romantic dinner. Xan returned her nod, then breathed a sigh of relief. She wouldn't have any exploding rock stars shouting around her house tonight. Still, she should check, to make sure.

Xan wound her way through the empty tables to where Jackie was scooping her dinner onto a plate. "Everything went okay?" Xan asked.

Jackie nodded again. "I left them having dessert. I'll go collect the table and everything after I've had my dinner."

Xan held up a halting hand. "Don't worry about it. I'll take care of it. I'll leave everything beside the path for Lee to collect in the morning. Time you knocked off for the night."

Wearily, Jackie thanked her and carried her plate to an

unoccupied table.

Xan breathed in the night air as she walked briskly to the eastern beach where Jay's elaborate setup still stood, though the couple had gone. Some of the candles had guttered out, but enough remained lit to show the heart-shaped stage they set. How sweet. She hadn't thought the rock star had any romance in him. Silently, she wished him luck for the rest of his evening as she disassembled the equipment from his dinner date. Within minutes, the folding table and chairs rested against a palm tree beside the path, with the dishes and folded tablecloth in a tub beside them. Next, she returned for the candles. A quick puff extinguished each one before she added those to the tub, too. The last item was an unopened bottle of wine, still sitting in the ice bucket, where they'd left it. She lifted the dripping bottle, debating whether to simply take it back to the hotel, or take it to the happy couple so she could check that they were, indeed, happy.

Xan's curiosity won...no, conscientiousness, she told herself, as she marched along the path back to Villa Penguin. She checked her wristband. Almost eight – moonrise. They wouldn't be inside yet, surely. Not with a magical staircase to see out here. Not that she'd ever had time to see it – standing around in the dark for hours, waiting for the moon to rise over the mudflats left behind by the retreating tide, while fighting off the mosquitoes trying to suck her dry...none of that really appealed to her. She'd much prefer a night dive.

But she was here now, with moonrise only minutes away. Standing at the foot of the jetty, she could just make out two shadows on the end, silhouetted against the rising moon. And it was magnificent. As orange as the sun, the moon rose from the waters, reflected across the waves and shallow pools in a series of steps that gave this phenomenon its name: Staircase to the Moon. The moon rose higher, paling from orange to gold, and the staircase extended closer to shore. Xan gasped in awe. She'd never seen anything like it. She didn't want to miss another one for as long as she lived here on the island. Truly magnificent.

"Nah, the battery's dead. You forgot to change it, didn't you? I told you!" a voice hissed, on the beach below.

"I did change it. It's not my fault it's not properly charged. I told you to make sure all the spares were fully charged, ready to go. Now we're missing it!" another voice whined.

Xan glanced up the jetty, where the two shadows had merged into one. Understanding morphed into annoyance as she slid down to the beach where the cameramen argued. "I told you not to film the guests! Get the hell out of here!" she roared, charging down the sand.

THIRTY-FIVE

Shouting broke the spell. One minute, Flavia was staring into Jay's eyes, parting her lips in anticipation of a magical kiss, then the next, she jumped to her feet, shaking her head.

What had she been thinking? Almost kissing him?

"Get the hell out of here!"

Flavia recognised the hotel manager's voice.

"We weren't filming them. We were getting footage of the moon," a male voice protested. Tim's, Flavia thought.

Her heart, a moment ago swelling to bursting at the thought of kissing Jay, froze. The film crew had been taking pictures of her again. Ones they could sell to the highest bidder to finance their future, while destroying hers.

"I want every memory card you have on you. Now," Ms Lane demanded.

Grumbling ensued, but Flavia couldn't focus on the

words through her fear. She wasn't safe out here. She wasn't safe from public scrutiny unless she stayed inside, away from Jay.

Flavia broke into a run, heading for the house. She swiped open the door and hurried to her room. Only with the door shut did she dare give in to her tears. With her knees and forehead pressed to the tiles, she sobbed her heart out. Romance and Jay and what had been a perfect night…shattered at the realisation that she couldn't have any of those things, or they'd cost her everything she loved in her life.

Some prices were too high to pay. Even for Jay Felix.

THIRTY-SIX

Fuck. What had he done wrong? Everything had been going so well, and now it was fucked.

"Thanks a lot," Jason snapped at Xan and her contractors as he bolted after Flavia. Fuck, but that girl could run. Must be those long legs she'd wrapped around his hips in the helicopter when he'd….fuck. That first time in the helicopter couldn't be their only time together. He'd stake his guitar on it.

"Flavia, wait!" he called, though he couldn't see her in the dark. For a second, he saw her silhouetted in the doorway of his villa before the door slid shut. At least she hadn't run off. Maybe he hadn't fucked everything up completely. Not yet, anyway.

He checked the rest of the house before he knocked on the closed guest room door. "Flavia?" he called softly, pressing his ear to the door. Did he hear sobbing? "Baby, are you okay?"

She sniffled. "Fine. I'm fine."

"Can I come in?" he ventured.

"No."

He debated for a second, before throwing caution to the wind. "Was it something I did?"

"No."

Jason breathed a sigh of relief. "So our date was all right, until they busted in on us?"

"The date was perfect until…they arrived." Another sniffle. "Jay, I'm tired. I just want to take a shower and get some sleep. All right?"

He nodded. "Fair enough."

It wasn't, though. None of this was fucking fair. Why couldn't people just leave them alone?

Jay headed to the lounge room and threw himself on the couch. He flicked on the TV, but all he got was blank screen. That's right, without a satellite dish, there weren't any TV channels. Throwing the remote control on the coffee table, Jason let out a string of every swear word he knew.

Wasn't he allowed to be as happy as anyone else? One date, that's all he'd asked for. And still they'd fucked it up for him. If he didn't know better, he'd swear Xan had deliberately messed this up for him. Out of jealousy, maybe. Except Xan didn't like him enough to be jealous. Revenge seemed more likely. He'd made her life difficult, so she was just returning the favour.

Damn it. If she wasn't such a good hotel manager, she'd be out on her ear.

Behind him, he heard Flavia's door crack open, then her

quiet footsteps until the bathroom door closed. It could have been any door, but he heard the lock click, confirming his guess.

The shower hissed and Jason imagined the water cascading over her naked body, her hands caressing her skin with the soap. If she was imagining him as clearly as he imagined her, her hands would slip between her thighs and she'd stroke herself until…

Flavia screamed. The shower screen rattled as she screamed again. A moment later, the bathroom door flew open and there she stood. Framed in the doorway, her eyes wide and wild, Flavia clutched a towel to her chest that she didn't have the presence of mind to wind around herself to hide those tempting curves peeking around the side of the white flannel.

She darted a fearful glance at the shower, then drew in a panting breath to scream again.

THIRTY-SEVEN

Jay jumped out of his seat as if the couch had bitten his bum. Maybe his bathroom wasn't the only part of his villa infested with too-friendly creatures. Flavia glanced at the shower and the sight of those green, clammy fingers which had climbed over her foot...she couldn't suppress another scream. She hated frogs. They were right up there with snakes as her least favourite animals.

"What's wrong?" he demanded.

Flavia skittered out of his way, keeping her back to the wall so he'd be between her and the little perverts. She pointed. "There are frogs in your shower!"

For a moment, Jay just stood there with his hands curled into claws like he was going to rip the things to shreds. Then, with a swift head shake, he yanked off his shirt and advanced into the shower. Using the shirt as a net, he snared one frog, twisted the fabric into a prison, and carried the whole bundle outside. He returned with the shirt dangling from one hand, a fierce expression on his face, and no sign of the first frog. The second frog managed to squirm free from his first attempt, and the second, but not the third. With considerable satisfaction, Jay transferred the final frog outside, too.

"Is that all of them?" Flavia asked fearfully, peering into the shower.

Jay spread his arms wide and shrugged. "Who knows? Fucked if I know how they get in here. There could be half a dozen more, all waiting their turn to shower with you. Or they could be saving themselves for me. Who knows about frogs and their sexual preferences?"

Flavia coughed out a laugh. Unknowingly, she'd saved herself for him. She had more in common with frogs than she'd realised. Didn't mean she wanted to continue showering with one.

Jay must have read her mind, because he flipped down the toilet seat and parked his bum on it. "I can sit here and guard you, if you like."

Flavia expected a sleazy look or at least a wink, but he just sat there, matter-of-factly, with his arms folded. She thought about refusing, or asking him to stand outside the bathroom door, but she felt safer with him in here. Yeah, he was a rock star who never said no to sex, but he was a gentleman who respected when a girl said no, too. At least, he had so far.

Feeling far too self-conscious in the presence of a man who'd already seen her naked, Flavia turned the shower on again. She didn't take her towel off until she stepped into the spray, and even then she hung it over the shower screen to partially hide her from sight. She'd almost finished rinsing the soap off her body when she caught movement out of the corner of her eye. She saw a flash of green and shrieked, flattening herself against the wall.

Jay burst into the shower, cornering the frog and shoving it back down the drain it had emerged from, before he stamped firmly on the drain cover.

Mere centimetres separated them, and Jay's shorts were soaked. If she had to choose between showering with a frog or a rock star, her choice was already made. She wrapped her arms around his neck and kissed him as hot water rained down on them both. Kissing Jay was like oxygen — one breath and she was hooked. Her heart hummed its approval and Jay…Jay just pulled her in close and made her forget everything except for the two of them, together.

Jay kissed his way down her breasts to the juncture of her thighs. Dear God, Jay Felix knelt at her feet, his lips kissing one thigh as his hand stroked the other. She parted for him, shivering as his fingers entered her.

"You said tonight was perfect. I can think of something that would make it even better. I want to hear you scream my name." Honey eyes trapped her gaze. "Would you like that?" One stroke of his finger sent a thrill deep inside her.

"Yes," she gasped, closing her eyes as she surrendered to sensation. God, he was good.

"On one condition. Don't close your eyes, baby. I want you looking at me every moment until you scream my name. Can you do that?"

She moaned, unable to utter coherent words any more, so she nodded.

Jay's gaze didn't leave hers as his fingers played her to

the point where she thought she'd combust.

"I want to taste you," he murmured, and his fingers were joined by his tongue.

Her knees turned to jelly at his pleasurable onslaught, but she didn't want him to stop. God no. She wanted him to continue drawing those tiny circles and rubbing her insides until she…until she…

"Oh God, Jay. Jay! I'm coming! I'm coming!"

He didn't stop. Even as she blew apart around him, he continued to weave a melody with his tongue that threatened to detonate her again. It shouldn't be possible. Not after such an incredible release. And yet…and yet…

Both a moment and an eternity passed.

"Jay! Oh my God! Jay!" she cried out.

If he hadn't held her upright, she'd have slid down the wall into a blissful puddle at his feet. Jay was a rock god and a sex god. No question.

"Now it's a perfect night." Jay wrapped a towel around her and helped her out of the shower.

Her blissful fog started to fade as she towelled herself dry. Yes, she was still tender from his touch, but she ached for more. How was that possible? Her eyes strayed to Jay, who stood in the middle of the bathroom in his wet clothes, grinning like that cat who got the canary. A very turned-on cat. Oh God, was he really that big? He'd fitted all that inside her yesterday?

"I should…help you do something with that," she faltered, waving in the direction of his groin.

Jay laughed, grabbing his dick through his shorts and leaving her with no illusions that every inch of that monster was his. "It's all right, baby. You're probably still sore from yesterday. I'll take care of it."

No. That wasn't right. He'd satisfied her…more than satisfied her. Didn't he deserve the same treatment?

Tucking her towel around her, Flavia helped him out of his soaked shorts, freeing the erection that was every bit as big as she'd feared. Not that it mattered for what she had in mind. This, she could handle. "No. Please, let me."

Mystified honey eyes regarded her as Jay gave his permission. That was all she needed.

She stroked his length with gentle fingers, each stroke firmer than the last, until it was Jay's turn to moan. Flavia smiled and licked her lips. Time to find out what rock star tasted like.

She took him into her mouth slowly, letting her tongue explore his head, the ridge around it, then his rock-hard shaft as she slid him deeper into her throat.

"Are you sure you're okay there? I'm big, and you're –"

His words ended in a heartfelt groan as Flavia demonstrated that she knew exactly what she was doing. The tip of her tongue touched his balls, she'd taken him so deep, but she didn't stop there. She fastened her hands on his hips and found her rhythm. Slow, languorous strokes as she sucked him in, raking her teeth over him oh-so-carefully on the way out. Jay wasn't the only one who could deliver unimaginable pleasure and she wanted to show him…thank him…for all of it.

She could feel him building to his climax, so it came as no surprise when he mumbled something incoherent about how he was going to blow. No, she was in control here, and she'd be the one to tip him over the edge. She timed it perfectly – she tasted raw rock star and revelled in the power she had over him at that moment. With his eyes closed and his mouth open, he looked like he'd seen heaven. Because of her.

Flavia allowed herself a smug smile as she crossed to the basin to clean herself up. It only took her a moment, by which time Jay looked like he'd recovered a bit. But only a bit.

"Fuck, Flavia. That has to be one of the best blowjobs I've ever had, and believe me when I say I know what I'm talking about. Don't tell me that was your first time."

She shook her head. "How do you think I managed to stay a virgin for so long?" She tightened the towel across her breasts and beat a hasty retreat to her room.

Once the door was firmly closed behind her, Flavia dropped to her knees. She'd broken another rule. They both had. And who was she kidding? She'd never given anyone but James a blowjob before, a man who'd always told her she needed more practice if she wanted to get really good at them, but Jay had said she was the best.

One thing was certain. James was a rotten liar and he didn't deserve her. But the real question was…did she deserve Jay Felix? Because she knew she wanted him, and her heart was waging a war against her head that she knew she couldn't win.

THIRTY-EIGHT

Jason had just sat down on the couch with his mid-morning coffee when the phone rang. Flavia was still fast asleep, so his first thought was to hope it didn't wake her, followed by a second, more alarming one: why the fuck was the phone ringing at all? Hadn't the helicopter crashed into the satellite dish and cut off all communications, phone and internet alike?

Bemused, he picked up the receiver. "Hello?"

"Finally. No, don't tell me what I interrupted. I don't want to know," Xan said.

Jason took a loud slurp from his cup. "Drinking coffee. Happy?"

"Surprised, maybe. That's all. I called to tell you the phones are fixed."

Jason snorted. "Yeah, I figured something weird was going on, when my broken phone rang. How?"

Xan laughed. "Call it a miracle, because I barely believe it myself. The guys at the pearl farm wanted a new satellite dish installed, so they called in some favours with the Abrolhos pearl farmers to find out who they use. Some communications technology wizard who can get them a better satellite uplink than most people in Perth. They lured the guy up here with his family for a holiday so he'd give them a quote. Turns out the guy's considering branching out into pearl farming, too, so he was in the dive boat, checking out the cages, when I radioed through yesterday. He turned up first thing this morning, skippering one of the dive boats like the King Sound whirlpools were just another day at the office. His wife's a fisher or something and makes him skipper their boat in all weather, so this was no worries."

Jason wasn't sure if he'd heard right. "A fisherman fixed the phones?"

"Sort of. He used to do mine site installations before he moved to the Abrolhos. Fishing's his wife's job. He just…fixes things. Like he fixed our satellite dish in less than an hour. Invoiced us on the spot, too – less than the usual guy, even with Sunday rates. He wouldn't stay for a coffee, though. He said he wanted to get back before his wife finished her morning swim."

"So your miracle repair man just vanished?"

"He was real, all right. He took Shou and the film crew with him when he left. Shou wanted to get back to arrange repairs for his helicopter, and the film crew had finished, so once we collected all their footage, I let them go." Xan sucked in a breath. "Hey, could you come up to IT to check it out? I want to be sure we identify anything that constitutes a privacy violation and delete it before we hand it all over to the advertising agency who'll manage the campaign. I'm talking about anything with you or your friend in it."

"Right now?"

"The sooner the better."

Jason swore, before agreeing to head up there in a minute.

He slammed the receiver down, wishing the phones weren't still working yet. He wanted to be here when Flavia woke up to ask her about last night. His dick wasn't going to forget it for a very long time, that was for sure. How had she known to....

"Morning," Flavia said with a nervous smile. "Did I hear the phone ring?"

Jason nodded. "Yeah. Xan got it fixed. Some fisherman or fisherman's husband or something. I dunno. But it works."

She swallowed. "Because I was supposed to fly out yesterday morning to see a friend and she's probably worrying about me, so if I could call her..."

"Sure." Jay pushed the phone toward her. "Go for it. I have to go out and watch some videos in the office. The film crew's gone home and the hotel manager wants me to make sure they haven't violated my privacy." He snorted. Like he'd let some bloke violate him.

"Really? Can you...make sure there aren't any naked pictures of me?" Flavia asked.

"Sure, baby." Especially if it meant looking at naked pictures of her to make sure. Whistling, Jason headed out to do a job that suddenly seemed a lot more fun than it had at first.

THIRTY-NINE

"Hello?" Violet's voice sounded suspicious.

"It's me. Flavia."

A squeal issued from the receiver. "Oh my God! I was ready to file a missing persons report. You weren't answering your phone, you haven't been on social media in days…All the girls want to know why you're not here yet. So, spill."

Flavia smiled faintly. How much to tell? "I'm all right. Honestly. No need to call the police. I might not make it to Bali, though. I got kind of caught up here and by the time I make it to the airport, I'd only have a day or two in Bali anyway. It wouldn't be worth it."

"So what kept you?" Violet demanded. "I worried that the auction guy went crazy after you cancelled the deal and kidnapped you, but you sound almost happy. Definitely not as down as you were when we left. Did you meet some hot man at the hotel and decide to have a dirty weekend?"

Flavia laughed. "Um, maybe."

"Spill!"

Flavia swallowed. Violet had been against the auction from the start. How could she tell her she'd gone through with it? "You know the auction guy?"

"You mean the dirty old man who wanted to chain you up in his basement?"

"He wasn't dirty or old. And he doesn't have a basement. No chains, either." Flavia surveyed the airy villa. She could even see the ocean sparkling through the window.

"But you still called off the deal, right? He took one look at your conditions and refused to go through with it?" Violet pressed.

Here it comes. Flavia took a deep breath. "No. He agreed to everything and signed without a murmur. He's gorgeous and rich and…a gentleman, too. Not a liar like James."

Violet gasped. "You did it with him, didn't you? Oh my God, you auctioned your body to a stranger! Did he get it over with really quickly, or did he draw it out? Is that why you haven't been able to get to an airport?"

Flavia felt her face grow hot. "He's not a stranger. Not any more. And I honestly don't know how long we took. It was…amazing. It's not like I was so bored that I was staring at my watch the whole time. The things he did to me, to my body…God, I thought I'd died and gone to heaven."

"You like him! I mean, really like like him! I wonder why he had to pay for sex, though, if he's so gorgeous and good in bed. Does he have some crazy secret that he doesn't want anyone to know? Like, does he have an weird shaped…you know…or a Hello Kitty tattoo on it, or does he have trouble getting it up, or – "

"NO! None of those things. I don't know, Vi. From the moment I met him, it was like none of this was about the money or the sex. It was like he wanted me, and the auction was just a way to get my attention. None of the rest of it mattered. He just said he wanted my first time to be special, and every moment was about making sure it was memorable for me. I…don't understand," Flavia admitted.

"So you and your sex god had sex, he paid you…and why aren't you here?"

Flavia sighed. She wasn't sure she could explain this. "We're kind of stuck on an island. Someone crashed the helicopter and we can't leave until it's fixed. I think there's a boat now, though, but it's left and I don't know when it'll be back. They said Tuesday."

"You're stranded on a desert island? How'd you get a hold of a phone? Hang on, did you guys have sex on the beach?"

Flavia played with her hair. Violet had to ask all the difficult questions. "I wanted to do it on the beach, but somehow we ended up doing it in the helicopter instead. And no, it's not a desert island. It has buildings and electricity and phones and everything, but they've been down since Friday so I couldn't call."

"You had sex in a helicopter? How is that even possible?"

Of course Violet would focus on that bit of information.

"I don't know, but it was incredible." Flavia was surprised to hear her voice sound so dreamy. "And then last night…"

"Wait. You had sex with him more than once? What about the agreement? The signed contract?"

"I ripped it up. He still gave me the money, though, and I don't know what to do with it. He doesn't have to pay for sex, Vi. He could have anyone. But he wanted me. And I want…" Her voice died to a whisper. "I think I've fallen for the guy who bought my virginity, Vi. What do I do?" Even as she said the words, Flavia knew they were true.

"He's gorgeous, and young, and incredible in bed. He wants you and he's made it clear. He's paid you the money, so he's not holding that over you. I can only imagine who this guy is. I mean, he sounds like Jay Felix, but there's no way a rock star like him would ever pay for sex. He has so many girls after him they'd pay him for sex, not the other way around." Violet laughed. She had no idea how right she was. "So, about your sex god. What do you want to do?"

"I want to follow my heart. But my heart says it belongs to a man who bought the rest of my body. That makes him no better than James, Vi."

A soft snort. "Girl, he's a million times better than James. I'll tell you what. Give him back the money, if that's the problem. Then enjoy the rest of your dirty weekend. I'll see you next week, when you can give me all the juicy details."

In a flurry of goodbyes, Violet hung up.

Flavia dropped the phone back in its cradle and stared at the handset as if it might hold more answers than she had right now.

Follow her heart. Enjoy the weekend. She liked him. Really liked him. All she had to do was give back the money and she'd be free to…what? Enjoy herself? It still didn't change anything, or the fact that Jay had paid her for sex, no matter how much she'd enjoyed it. And what if Jay didn't want to do it again?

But all the trouble he'd gone to last night, with the romantic dinner on the beach, and the moonlight, and the wine, and then last night saving her from the frogs and afterwards…no, Jay was nothing like James. But the money…that really was the sticking point. What would Jay say when she tried to give it back to him? She couldn't keep it. Just the thought of that money made her feel cheap.

She could never be with a man who paid women for sex. Never.

Unless…

An idea sparked in her mind. Maybe there was a way to give back the money, and get what she wanted. What did she have to lose?

Just her heart.

FORTY

The automatic door hissed open and Flavia glanced up from her book. She was sure she couldn't remember a single word she'd read, but she'd needed some sort of distraction while she was waiting for Jay to return. And now…here he was. She swallowed. It was now or never.

"It's a beautiful day out here, and the tide's just coming in. How about another walk on the beach?" Jay asked.

Flavia was tempted, but she had to be sure. "Are those men with cameras gone?"

Jay laughed. "Yeah, they left on a boat this morning. So no paparazzi taking pictures. Just us. What do you say?"

Mutely, Flavia nodded. She set her book on the coffee table and padded barefoot after Jay. The ladder was warm under her hands as she descended to the same beach where they'd shared dinner last night. There was no sign of the table, candles or anything else now, though – the spot where Jay had kindled a fire in her heart over dinner and a flaming dessert was now under water, the sand barely visible through the milky blue sea.

Would Jay wipe away the memories of last night just as easily? Flavia's hand flew to her pocket and the envelope nestled there. Yes, she was doing the right thing, she reassured herself.

"Penny for your thoughts?" Jay said.

She swallowed. "I was thinking about all the things we've done together. On Friday and…last night. And how much I enjoyed it."

Jay grinned. "Me, too. Hey, you never did get doggy-style on the beach like you wanted. We could do it here."

"No!" It came out more harshly than she'd intended. "No. I don't think I'll ever be able to get on my hands and knees again without remembering that. Not one of the memories I want to rehash in a hurry."

Jay shrugged. "Fair enough. Wasn't my finest moment, either."

Flavia took a deep breath. "I was thinking…after last night, I have something to ask you."

"Will I marry you? But I barely know you, baby. This is very sudden." Though he looked serious, Jay's wink gave him away.

Flavia laughed. "Um, not really. I'm not sure I'm the marrying kind. Not any more. No, what I have in mind is more of a business proposition." She pulled the envelope out of her pocket and smoothed it. Jay's eyes lit with recognition.

"That's not enough to buy my hotel, and I'm not interested in selling," he said.

Flavia licked her lips. He sure wasn't making this easy for her. But she had to do it. "I'm not interested in your hotel. I'm interested in you. I'd like to make you an offer. This for…one more time with you. For you to make me feel like a million dollars again." She held out the envelope, praying he'd take it.

Jay extended his hand and plucked the envelope from her fingers. He whipped out the letter with the numbered account and its balance, then squinted at it. "That's a lot of money for one time, even with a rock star. I'd have some conditions on a deal like that."

Flavia sighed in relief. At least he'd accepted the money from her, for the moment. "And your conditions are?"

"Well, I think this would buy you more than just one round of sex. After all, you're hardly my first."

Flavia nodded. She wouldn't complain about more time with Jay.

"Not to mention a lot of kissing and foreplay. No sex without both of those."

She smiled. "All right."

"I'm not finished yet. The time you spend with me, it's not over until you're completely satisfied. And I get to show you how sex on the beach should really be done." He peered over the page. "Do you agree?"

"Yes. Then we'll be even," Flavia said.

Jay shook his head. "No, this doesn't make us even. To be even, I'd have to give you more than one night. Maybe a week, at least. Or even longer. I'd want to give you your money's worth, baby. So what do you think?"

She breathed out all her tension and beamed. "It sounds wonderful, Jay. When do we start?"

He pulled her into his arms. All other thoughts vanished as he claimed her mouth for a kiss that promised happily ever after. "Right now, baby. After the first time, it only gets better and better."

The story continues in
The Rock Star and the Billionaire

ABOUT THE AUTHOR

Demelza Carlton has always loved the ocean, but on her first snorkelling trip she found she was afraid of fish.

She has since swum with sea lions, sharks and sea cucumbers and stood on spray drenched cliffs over a seething sea as a seven-metre cyclonic swell surged in, shattering a shipwreck below.

Demelza now lives in Perth, Western Australia, the shark attack capital of the world.

The *Ocean's Gift* series was her first foray into fiction, followed by her suspense thriller *Nightmares* trilogy. She swears the *Mel Goes to Hell* series ambushed her on a crowded train and wouldn't leave her alone.

Want to know more? You can follow Demelza on Facebook, Twitter, YouTube or her website, Demelza Carlton's Place at:

www.demelzacarlton.com

Books by Demelza Carlton

Ocean's Gift series

Ocean's Gift (#1)
Ocean's Infiltrator (#2)
Ocean's Depths (#3)
Water and Fire

Turbulence and Triumph series

Ocean's Justice (#1)
Ocean's Trial (#2)
Ocean's Triumph (#3)
Ocean's Ride (#4)
Ocean's Cage (#5)
Ocean's Birth (#6)
How To Catch Crabs

Nightmares Trilogy

Nightmares of Caitlin Lockyer (#1)
Necessary Evil of Nathan Miller (#2)
Afterlife of Alana Miller (#3)

Romance Island Resort series

Maid for the Rock Star (#1)
The Rock Star's Email Order Bride (#2)
The Rock Star's Virginity (#3)
The Rock Star and the Billionaire (#4)

Mel Goes to Hell series